Born to Trot

Born to Trot

By MARGUERITE HENRY

Illustrated by Wesley Dennis

RAND McNALLY & COMPANY

NEW YORK • CHICAGO • SAN FRANCISCO

*The characters in this story are real
and to them* BORN TO TROT *is dedicated*

To the man
> Benjamin Franklin White, the
> dean of colt trainers, and four-
> time winner of the Hambletonian.

To the boy
> Gibson White, owner of Rosalind,
> and son of "Hambletonian Ben."

To the filly
> Rosalind, world champion trotting mare, 1:56¾;
> record in double harness with Greyhound, 1:58¼.

Born to Trot

One

THE sun was no more than a pink promise. Yet the first horses were already skimming the track, legs winking blackly against the white fence. In the half haze of morning the spider-web sulkies barely could be seen. The drivers seemed floating along on the outflung tails of their horses.

In the vast, deserted grandstand a lone boy was scratching the head of his old dog, Bear. The boy was in his early teens, tall for his age, lean and rangy, with eyes dark except for flecks of golden light in them. As he patted Bear, he gave no sign that he was thinking of the dog at all. His eyes were rounding the track with the trotters and pacers, and there was a look of awareness in them—as if something had long been brewing inside him and now was ready to boil over.

"Morning, Pony Boy!" A jovial voice cut across his thoughts and a roughened hand tweaked his ear. "How come you're not out there on the track working your pony?"

Gibson turned and saw the old horseman, Bill Dickerson.

Pony Boy! That was it—Pony Boy! The name rankled. He was tired of forever jogging his pony up the stretch instead of down the stretch, tired of getting nowhere. Even the pony must be bored with the monotonous, treadmill sort of work. Even he might get to thinking less of himself for it. Suddenly, right there in the grandstand while the horses flew past him and while the old reinsman waited an answer, the boy was struck with a knowing. He knew he belonged with the horses and men skimming through the morning light. He felt himself old enough to take a green colt as they had done, to train him on and on until life for that colt was all smooth-flying trot.

Bill Dickerson stood grinning, putting on his gloves, adjusting his racing goggles. Gibson realized the man had not meant to belittle him. "I'm going to hitch up my pony now," he answered at last.

But instead of moving off at once, he waited, watching the famous reinsman step out on the track where a groom stood holding a nervous mare. He watched the old legs arc over the sulky seat, heard the soft voice cluck to the mare, saw her strike up a trot. Then he lost them all to the mist.

Troubled over his problem, he came down out of the grandstand and trudged slowly toward his father's stable. Bear sniffed on ahead, stopping occasionally to growl at a pet goose or to chase a bantam rooster.

Beyond the stables in a shaded paddock Tony, a sturdy pinto, stood rubbing himself against the bark of a tree, trying to shed the last of his winter coat.

At the sound of Gibson's whistle Tony left off his scratching and loped over to the gate. He knew each day's routine. First the grooming, then the harnessing. Then the cart pulled up behind him and the shafts made snug in the harness straps.

Usually Gibson talked to Tony while he brushed and buckled and tied, but this morning he worked in broody silence. He felt tired, somehow. Only Bear was excited as ever, yapping

11

and dancing on his hind legs to lick the pony's face. It was one thing, Gibson told himself, to know with a piercing sureness that you were hard-muscled and ready to do a man's work, but it was another thing to convince your father. Not that Tony isn't the best in the world, he thought as he checked the shaft straps, giving a pull to see if they were tight. It's just that a fellow outgrows things. First he outgrows his little Shetland. Then he gets too big for his cow pony. And suddenly he's ready for a big-going horse.

"What's the matter, boy?" The words came low-pitched from a groom washing leg bandages. "You ain't chatting to that pony of yours this morning." The voice drawled, going up and down with the sudsing. "What's the matter?"

"We're both thinking, Jim. That's all."

"Ho-ho-ho! Tony don't think nothing but oats." Then Jim cut his laughter short as he saw Gibson really was thinking. His glance followed after them as boy and dog climbed into the training cart and Tony trotted off toward the red mile, important as any big horse.

The sun was more than a promise now. It was up and about its business—gilding the knobs of the quarter poles, firing fence rails, gathering up dew from the grass in the centerfield.

Gibson started jogging Tony up the stretch. The big trainers started their horses the same way. Three times the wrong way around at a slow jog, then the right way, spinning faster and faster with each mile. Tony, of course, never went the right way of the track at all; he might interfere with the big horses. His workout was humbug. Only make-believe.

For the moment the boy's problem fell away. It was good to be alive on a Kentucky spring morning. Bear must have thought so, too. He grinned from ear to ear, not minding at all that his paws kept slipping down between the slats of the rig.

One by one the drivers, including Gibson's father, passed and waved hello. A meadow lark on a tree stump whistled a string of silver notes. But to the boy the most exciting music was the snare-drum roll of hoofbeats, the trotters picking them up, putting them down, tap-tap, tap-tap, playing their own fanfare to the day.

"Say, Gib!" It was Driver Tom Berry coming up from behind. "Dickerson and I are having an argument. He says you've been working Tony two years. I say three. Which is it?"

Gibson thought a moment. "Four," he replied, biting his lip.

"When are you going to retire him?" Tom Berry laughed in amusement. And he was off in a cloud of red dust that set the pony to sneezing and the boy to coughing.

Shamefaced, Gibson drew rein and headed back to the paddock. He felt the drivers' eyes following him off the track, imagined them laughing behind their goggles. I'd rather they laughed out like Tom Berry! he thought.

With slow, deliberate fingers he unhitched Tony and turned him loose. Then with extra care he cleaned the harness —the collar and girth and crupper and reins. Each piece he soaped and wiped and oiled and stored away in a harness bag. He wiped the cart next, each spoke of each wheel, until it was clean and shining as Tony's bit. In every move there was finality.

A groom looked up, puzzled. "Quitting early?"

Gibson nodded in silence. Then he walked slowly back to the track, pulled by some invisible lead strap. He sat on a tree stump there, feeling tired and lonely. And although his head was bent, watching his boot make a groove along the ground, he was conscious of the horses whisking by, of the drivers glancing casually in his direction. He read their thoughts.

"There sits Pony Boy."

"Why isn't he driving that cute pony of his?"

Mr. White's assistant, Guy Heasley, came up now, talking more to the horse he was leading than to Gibson. "Man, oh man! Lookit Ben steppin' that filly along!"

Guy Heasley always seemed to know just when to come, just when Mr. White was ready to exchange a worked horse for one that needed working.

Watching his father dismount, Gibson wondered why the newspapers lumped his name with the veteran drivers. His shoulders were not rounded, and even though his hair was almost white, his step was sure and easy, as if time never bossed him.

Instead of exchanging horses, Mr. White asked Guy Heasley to hold both a moment. Then, slow-paced, he sauntered over to Gibson. "Son, Alma Lee should be worked another mile. Want to hold the lines over a real trotter?"

Gibson seemed rooted to the stump. He didn't trust his voice. Had his father read his mind?

"Her sire won the Kentucky Futurity," Mr. White was saying. "She's a chip off the old block." Then, taking the answer to his question for granted, he placed his own stop watch in Gibson's hand.

With that, the boy was on his feet, the golden flecks in his eyes dancing. "Mean it, Dad?" he asked, showing a quick look of gratitude.

"Yes, Son."

"How much shall I go?"

"Let her step the mile in two-ten. It won't hurt her."

"Should I do the first half in one-five?"

"You can't always go each half in the same time. Just try to step her home in two-ten. Go down an eighth of a mile, then come up ready to score and get her away flying. This half-mile pole can be the starting line." Mr. White turned to Guy Heasley. "You work the fresh horse, Guy. I want to watch Gib."

Sixty-six seconds at the half pole! He was part of the horse as if he were astride; yet he could watch her action too—the propelling power of hocks, the long, low way of going. And all of this power he controlled with a feather touch. If he were unsteady, she might break into a run. Steady . . . steady. One-two, three-four.

Ninety-nine seconds at the three-quarter pole! Now a horse and sulky blocked his way. They must not pocket him. This was a brush against time. Only thirty-one seconds left! He guided Alma Lee away from the rail and they sailed along-side the other horse. Now the two horses were trotting as if hitched together. Gibson looked at the whip tilting in the wind but did not use it. Instead, he made the chirruping sound he had often heard his father use. It was better than a whip! It was a low question. And Alma Lee answered. She swept by the other horse. She passed the finish line and Gibson clicked his stop watch. The hands pointed to 2:09¾.

And with that click he broke out in a cold sweat. He pulled Alma Lee to a stop and circled back toward his father. Mr. White was not alone now. Several drivers and grooms clus-tered about, comparing the time. And behind them sat the rail-birds, the people who came to watch the early morning work-outs. Gibson jumped out of the sulky. He pointed to the hands of the watch and waited eager-eyed for some word from his father.

But Mr. White said nothing. He was moving off, ready to work another horse.

"Cool Alma Lee out slowly, Son," he called back as he mounted the sulky. "Then come to the office."

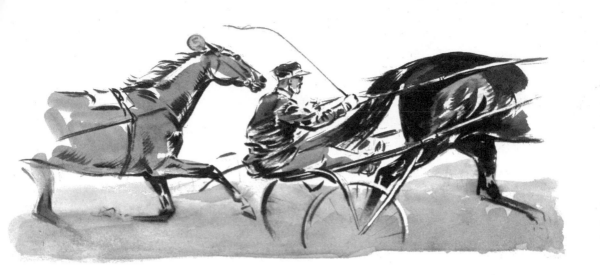

Two

"COOL her out slowly!" That would mean two hours. Washing. Scraping. Rubbing. Walking her. Two hours before he would know. Did his father think him still a boy, able only to manage a pony? Or did he see him a reinsman at last, arms and legs muscled, hands strong and firm?

As Gibson unbuckled Alma Lee's harness, his mind raced on into summer. Summer meant the Grand Circuit, the "big league" of harness racing. Oldtimers called it the Big Apple, joking about it, thumbing and snapping their suspenders as they told how they traveled the little pumpkin fairs before they were dry behind the ears, and how they trained on and on until their horses graduated to the Big Apple.

He took off Alma Lee's bridle and put on her halter, his mind still busy. The Big Apple! The Grand Circuit! Hopscotching from one state to another. Crisscrossing back and forth. Maine to Missouri. Ohio to California. Illinois to New York. And in New York, the Hambletonian, the biggest trotting race in the world. Would his father think he was ready for the Grand Circuit this summer?

He crosstied Alma Lee and ran into the stable with an empty pail. For a moment he paused. All over the country, wherever he went, there would be stables just like this one. And near by, Bill Dickerson's, Tom Berry's, Fred Egan's, and all the others. And beyond the stables, the track, smooth and beckoning.

He hung his pail on the nozzle of the faucet, letting the water run, now from the hot tap, now from the cold. "Must be milk-warm," he said to himself, plunging his hand into it. He added more cool water, tested again. Now it was right. He reached into the salt box and scooped up a big lump. Then he made a long-handled spoon of his arm and swished the salt around and around in the water until it dissolved.

He ran back to Alma Lee, the water spilling and splashing. The grooms looked up from their own work and smiled. They were proud of Gibson. They felt he belonged to their world of horses and men.

"Clean sponges are dryin' out there in the sun," one of them called, pointing a finger to the odd-shaped lumps on the grass.

Gathering up the biggest, Gibson put a question to Guy Heasley. "Did Dad say anything to you?"

"No, that he didn't." Guy shook his head, rubbing his thin nose. "He's not one to run off with words when maybe his mind ain't even made up."

It was true, and no one knew it better than Gibson. He began sponging Alma Lee, sloshing the water over her back, her barrel, her dust-caked belly, over her quarters and down her legs. A steam rose from her body, bringing out the good

horse smell. He took the scraper and ran it lightly over her neck, heavier along her barrel. Alma Lee leaned against it instead of away from it. Again and again he scraped, squeezing the water from her coat.

Then he brushed and wisped and threw a woolen blanket over her, pinning it underneath like a fond parent tucking a child in bed. When he had given her a small drink of water, he began walking her around and around—past the stalls with velvet noses reaching out, past the lookers-on in front of the stables.

Some of the men leaned forward in their camp chairs, eagerly clocking their favorite horses, going the mile with them. Some were owners with a kind of longing in their eyes, wishing perhaps they were drivers or trainers or even stable-boys. And some were just lonesome, retired men who sat heavily in their chairs, letting the sun mottle their hands.

Gibson usually had a quick smile for them and often stopped to answer a question about Tony or Bear. But this morning his mind was at work, planning how he would ask his father, trying to find words as strong as his wanting. Around and around he walked, past grooms hanging leg band-ages up to dry, past pets of every description—cats and dogs and goats and geese and strutting little banties. And out on the track he could see his father changing horses again, stop-ping first to talk to the new horse before taking up the reins.

Gibson's heart beat high. He felt a bursting pride in this well-ordered world. Here, the long rows of stables with their tidy array of blankets and brooms and baskets and trunks. And beyond, the track running in a smooth oval, and the grandstand with its climbing tiers of seats. And over it all the rhythmic beat of hoofs.

He heard a big-lunged driver singing hymns to his horse at the top of his voice. Gibson half envied the man. He wanted to sing, too, but only scraps of song came into his mind— scraps that didn't belong together. Right now, if he started to sing, the words and the tunes would be all mixed up until a hybrid song came out, like "Jesus loves me, this I know, Ee-ai, ee-ai, oh!" He didn't mean it at all the way it would sound. So he did not sing aloud. Inside him, however, there was often a kind of music going. It sprang up now as he walked Alma Lee. And out on the track this morning there had been such a terrible ecstasy in him that the music was all trumpets and bugles, with a deep bassoon to mark his growing up.

Keep walking. Slower, he reminded himself. Slower still. Get the tension out of her. Walk over cinder paths. Over new green grass. Change the heavy plaid blanket for a lighter one. Walk until your head nods up and down like Alma Lee's.

Give her another small drink of water. Change the blanket again, a lighter one still. Keep walking. Seconds. Minutes. Another half hour. Now slide a hand under her blanket, against the coat of Alma Lee.

Cooled out at last! Her coat satin to his touch, as if she had never been worked at all. He took her to her stall, watched her bunt a mound of hay and tear out a mouthful. She was ready to eat. Yes, he had cooled her out slowly.

With long strides he made for the office of the stable, then slowed his steps. He stopped and took a breath before he pulled the door open. At sound of the creaky noise, his father looked up. He was alone, sitting at the plain old desk with its little pile of bills and papers and an open ink bottle and the plate that Gibson's mother kept filled with fruit.

Mr. White's eyes went over the boy, noticing the wet shirt flat against his ribs.

"Time you were getting cooled out yourself," he smiled, motioning toward the closed door at the end of the room. "Take your shower first. Then we'll talk."

Gibson walked through the sparely furnished office, drumming his fingers along the trunk under the window, along the cot against the wall, and the few camp chairs. His bath took far less time than Alma Lee's. Clothes skinned off in a trice. The shower needling him, first hot, then cold. Then on with the dry shirt his mother always left there.

Refreshed and a little breathless, he opened the door and stood before his father, waiting.

Mr. White half turned in his chair. He sat pensively a few moments. Then his blue eyes caught and held the brown ones of Gibson. "Son," he said slowly, "training trotters is a strange and wonderful profession."

The boy stood quiet, listening with every fiber.

"The trainer is the wind. With the breath of his own life he blows upon the sapling colt. He bends it in the way he wants it to grow, never breaking it."

Excitement caught at Gibson. These were words he understood.

The voice went on. "Half of a horse's gameness and speed is in the brain of his trainer."

Back in the stable a horse neighed sharply and the sound touched off answering whinnies.

"It was a good mile you drove this morning, Son. You have a light, neat touch upon the reins. I am proud."

The boy's sigh came from deep within. He reached for one of the apples on the plate, not because he was hungry but because he needed something to hold in his hand.

"*If,*" Mr. White hung on the little word a long time, "if you were to go along on the Grand Circuit this summer, what would you do about Tony?"

Gibson replied quickly. "I'd give him to a young boy, Dad. Tony's tired of jogwork. He needs a change—country roads with rabbits and squirrels popping out at him."

"Then you'd like to go with me?"

Blood climbed hot in Gibson's cheeks. "Oh, Dad! All morning I've been figuring how to ask you." Then a question crossed his face.

Mr. White answered as if the words had been spoken. "No," he replied gently, "not in a real race. Owners wouldn't mind your handling the lines in the workouts, but in a race they'd object to a green driver." He picked up a pencil and whittled a fine point. "This morning was hardly a test, Son. Alma Lee is a trained and sensible mare. Just because . . ." The words were left dangling.

Gibson twirled the woody stem so fiercely that the apple thudded to the floor. "Jogging around the track is fun for

a while, Dad," he said, frowning, "but it's not the real thing. At school we practice and drill in track and basketball and football just so we can compete with other schools. Training hard wouldn't be any fun if it didn't go on to a contest. That's what's important."

"I know what you mean, Gib, but it takes time." Mr. White let his eyes measure the boy. "You're slim as a colt and just as spindle-legged." In fact, you're downright gaunt, he thought but did not say.

He did say, "Your mother and I think you're trying to do too much, poking too many fingers in too many pies. Boxing. Track. Baseball. Football. Basketball. Everything."

"Not everything, Dad. Not tennis or swimming. But maybe next year . . ."

"We're hoping that going along with me on the Grand Circuit will make you let up a bit, will make you a better feeder, too, and put a little weight on you."

Gibson let himself sink down onto the solidness of the trunk. A far-off look came into his eyes. "The Grand Circuit!" he whispered, letting his thoughts run away. One-two, three-four. Never a skip or a break. Hard little hoofs drum-beating for the lead. Tap-tap, tap-tap. He could hear them already.

Three

LOADING horses. Shipping them. Unloading them. A strange city every week, but a good at-home feeling in each one. Everywhere the neat stables row on row, the clean rye straw, the good-smelling hay. Everywhere the clay mile in the sun. Everywhere the horses. And Gibson jogging them both ways of the track now. Slow. Fast. Faster. Around and around. Eating dust. Sweating and steaming with the horses. Week in, week out. This was the Grand Circuit.

From the moment the sun nosed above the horizon until it sailed high overhead, the hours flew. Mornings, Gibson was one of the men, a driver working alongside the big trainers, alongside his father and Bill Dickerson, Tom Berry and the others. They accepted him without question.

But in the afternoons he was a boy again and his world stood empty. Then the trainers drove in real races while he hung on the outside rail looking on—wanting to know risk and rivalry, wanting to match skill for skill, wanting to belong. Age seemed to be required, he thought bitterly. If you had white hair you could compete. Otherwise you were still a boy, not to be taken seriously. You could only watch while your father and all the others drove.

And watching, the longing in him sharpened. There was something in the way the men crouched close to their horses and clucked or sang to them that made him long fiercely to be out there, too. He felt it most when they reached the far turn and began the brush down the stretch. Then he had to lean hard against the fence to hold his feelings in. He wanted to be in on the brush, to cluck and talk and telegraph his strength to his horse.

What fun was it to tune up in the morning? It was like being part of a big orchestra during rehearsals. Then when the curtain went up and the signal was given, you were shunted off to one side to sit with the audience.

It had been the same way in school last fall. Always he was on the second team, always sitting on the bench waiting to hear his name called out. And then dusk, and the game over, and his name still uncalled.

And so the days were divided, the mornings important, the afternoons waste. Gibson tried to busy himself during the races—in the blacksmith tent where the ringing sound of the sledge killed the tap-tap, tap-tap music of the trotters; in his father's office making endless lists of trotters and pacers with their record time for the mile. But it was no use. He might as well be fiddling with blocks and beads.

Even while he wrote or while he helped the smith, his mind was out there on the far turn. And always some inner timing drew him to the track just when the horses were flying down the stretch. Eagerly his eyes would pick and choose until he found one in the ruck, and with clenched fists he would *will* that horse to win. Sometimes the game little trotter did win, inching his way forward, overhauling horse after horse until he was on top and the crowd screaming and cheering him on. Sometimes he came in only second or third, but in the boy's mind he, himself, was always handling the lines, playing the horse along for the best he had in him.

One afternoon in late summer Gibson was idling his time in the blacksmith tent, watching the smith cushion a hoof against pain. He did not see or hear anyone enter. Suddenly his father was spinning him around, saying in quick, sharp words, "Son! Johnny Struthers can't drive in the next heat. We can use you."

"Well, I'm a greenhead fly!" The blacksmith was first to find his voice. "You'll be about the only driver in the Grand Circuit who ain't a graybeard," he laughed, slapping his stomach.

Gibson nodded, his dark eyes throwing back the yellow sparks of the forge.

Four

GIBSON was off down the cinder path to the stable, head straining forward as if it couldn't wait for his feet to catch up.

"You'll be up behind Rocco." his father was explaining, trying to keep abreast. "You've never driven him before, but he's steady as they come." His eyes were merry as he asked, "How does it feel to be a catch driver, Son?"

"Catch driver?" Gibson did not slacken pace, only turned his head.

"Mmm. It's an old name for a young fellow who catches a bit of luck like this."

"Like a sub called from the bench?"

"Exactly. But catch drivers are most always gifted. They've

got horse sense. Seem to know what a horse is going to do before he does it."

Back in Mr. White's office Johnny Struthers' racing silks hung on pegs, the jacket bellying out in the middle as if the man himself were still inside. Gibson slipped it on, fidgeting with impatience while his father lapped over the belt and fastened it with a horse-blanket pin. His eyes darted out of the office window, watching the grooms hitching up for the next race, watching the horses of earlier races cooling out, hearing the hum of the crowd, feeling the excitement, seeing the wide, empty track beckoning, beckoning.

He looked toward his father, hoping for a word of advice, but again Mr. White had nothing to say. Only the eyes smiling, as if all had been said or done a long time ago.

With Johnny Struthers' cap pressed on his head, Gibson knelt down on the trunk, let his father pin it to size. Now the goggles. Now gloves pulled over sweating hands. Now Guy Heasley's stubbled face in the door and his voice calling out, "Ready! Time for you both to be parading to the post!" His eye ran over Gibson, winking encouragement.

Somewhere near the grandstand the band played a fanfare, the voice of the bugles helping Gibson into the sulky, braving his hands on the reins. Then the music stopped and the announcer's words tore into the quiet. "In seventh position, young Gib White driving for Johnny Struthers."

Gibson heard his name called out, but it seemed far off, as if it belonged to a stranger. His eyes were on Rocco's head. I've got to keep him looking straight forward. I've got to feel his mouth, telegraph to him. I've got to keep him on the trot, never letting him break. I want to get in the thick of it. I've got to!

They were scoring for the word now, approaching the starter, horses and drivers impatient to get on their way. And suddenly they were at the starting line and the word "Go" was a pistol shot.

Gibson felt Rocco gathering force. Now he was in the pack and part of the pack with the wind running along his cheeks and past his ears and into them, and his hold on the reins strong and steady. He was of the horse, one with the horse, one with his flight.

On either side, and in front and behind, he could hear the thunder of hoofs and the drivers clicking and clucking and coaxing and shouting. He could feel Rocco going up to the bit, straining against it, quickening his action.

The field was starting to bunch as they approached the turn. Soon Gibson would find a needle's eye and thread Rocco through it. Together they would burn a hole to the front.

And then at the first turn, with the race barely begun, Gibson felt his right arm jerk violently backward, saw the rein go slack in his hand. It had snapped in two! He had no control over his horse. His hand froze to the useless line and a cold knife of fear twisted within him. He glanced around, saw the field converging down on him. A bad pile-up flashed in his mind. Locked wheels. Sulkies capsized. Drivers tossed high. Horses on top of men. His father among them.

In the split second of its happening Rocco knew he was driverless. The torn rein frilled along his neck, egging him on, loosing his head in the way he wanted to go. He broke from his trot into a mad gallop, jerking toward the inside rail, poking holes in the pack where there were none, missing sulkies by thin whispers, going for the rail.

The whip! This was the time for it. Gibson cracked it

sharply to the left, trying to send Rocco to the outside rim, away from the onrushing field. Instead, the sound took the stallion by surprise, sent him heading straight for a crash with Tom Berry. But by some miracle the wheel hubs only grazed each other in a steely whine.

Maddened by his speed, Rocco veered closer and closer to the fence, magnetized by it. Gibson saw the top rail, higher than most and razor sharp. If Rocco plunged against it, he might be decapitated. And all the while Gibson could hear the field pounding along, narrowing down on him. Now twin jets of steam were whistling down his neck. From the corner of his eye he saw the horse behind. It was his father's!

Frantic, Gibson snaked the whip on Rocco's left, but again Rocco defied it, swerving ever closer to the rail. He would surely upset his father's horse unless . . . unless . . . Horse sense! You've got to know what a horse is going to do before he does it.

There was only one way to stop him—leap on his back, ride him away. With no thought for his own safety, Gibson grabbed the crupper under Rocco's tail, pulled himself forward, vaulted onto the horse's back.

Now the boy was astride a hurricane, wrenched forward, backward, slithering from side to side. He tried to grip Rocco with his knees, but the shafts of the sulky spread his legs far apart. Three times he reached for the loose rein and three times Rocco turned on a fresh blast of speed, jerking it out of his hand.

The breath racked out of the boy, and almost at the end of his strength he grabbed once again. He had it! With a quick pull on the bridle he steered Rocco away from the rail just as his father's horse skinned by.

Pulling, releasing, pulling, Gibson brought the panicky horse to a stop on the outside rim. The color gone from his face, he dismounted, and step by step led Rocco, still hitched to the sulky, toward the gate.

For a full minute the announcer's voice was unable to penetrate the hysterical screams from the grandstand. Then a hush of relief fell on the crowd and the announcer made the most of it. "Ladies and gentlemen! You have just witnessed the most courageous feat in Grand Circuit history. From the first quarter Rocco, the number seven horse, was a runaway with a broken rein. Young Gib White jumped on his back to avoid a tragic pile up. He risked his life not only for the safety of others, but for the welfare of his horse."

A clamor rose from the grandstand, applause and cheers. But to Gibson the cheers were just a blur of noise; they gave him no comfort. He turned his face and hid it in Rocco's mane. Here he was on the outer rim. On the outside again.

Would he never compete in a real race?

Five

WHEN the races were over that afternoon, the stream of people flowing out of the grandstand divided. Some poured into the parking lot and out of the gate. Some rushed to Tom Berry's stable, eager to see and perhaps even to touch the winner that had trotted the fastest race of the day. But many sought Gibson White. They trailed up and down with him as he walked the excitement and tension out of Rocco. They hurled questions at him, poked their cameras at him, at Rocco.

Thinking of the horse, Gibson kept right on walking. He plowed through the crowd, answering questions in monosyllables, wishing the day were done.

And then it was over, and he and his father were alone in their hotel room and it was night. But there was no sleep in them. The sound of automobile horns came up to them, and of trucks straining to climb the hill in front of the hotel, and of gears scraping as tired drivers tried to make the next town.

The room still held the heat of the day, curtains hanging limp at the open window, sheets hot to the touch, as if they had just been ironed.

Gibson smothered a cough.

In the bed on the other side of the night table, Mr. White stirred. "Gib—?"

"Yes, Dad."

A pause, then slow words, measured. "You probably saved my life today."

Gibson blotted the sweat trickling down his chest. "What do you mean?"

"Rocco was really my entry, but at the last minute I switched and gave him to you. Figured he'd be easier to handle."

A silence closed them in. Then, "Honest, Dad?"

Mr. White chuckled softly. "Honest as I'm lying here on this hot skillet of a bed. I doubt if I could've chinned myself up on Rocco's crupper the way you did. Rocco and I both would have landed on that fence rail."

Again the silence, then the words, "Thanks, Son."

All Gibson answered was, "Gosh, Dad, it wasn't anything." He locked his hands behind his head and looked up at the light flashing on the ceiling from the theater across the street. A sigh of contentment escaped him. Now he didn't mind at all the way his first race had ended.

After a while Mr. White broke the spell. His voice was troubled. "You hardly touched your dinner tonight, Son."

"Just not hungry, Dad."

"You've been coughing."

"It's the car fumes from the street."

"I don't mean just tonight."

A note of irritation crept into Gibson's voice. "I tell you, Dad, I'm all right."

"Maybe you are, Son, but with your mother not here I can't take chances. She wanted you to gain weight this summer, not lose it. We'll see a doctor in the morning." Gibson felt the quiet words firm, knew his father's eyes were steel blue now. "I've been inquiring. There's a good clinic here. Maybe," he said almost as an afterthought, "if the doc says you're all right, you can drive Expectation tomorrow. Johnny Struthers may be out tomorrow, too. Now will you sleep?"

Sleep! How could he sleep with the prospect of driving again? This time he would test the stitching on the reins, test every piece of leather. This time it would be different. He wiped the beads of perspiration from his upper lip. "I'll try to get to sleep. And thanks, Dad."

Mr. White brought a pitcher of cold water and a glass and set them on the night table. "Maybe this'll help," he said as he crawled back into bed.

Gibson sat up and poured himself a drink. He took a long time sipping it and when he had set the glass on the tray, he fell asleep at once.

Morning came, and with it a gray drizzle that would grease the track. As Gibson pulled on his clothes he knew the horses couldn't be worked. He was glad. If he had to go to the clinic, he would miss nothing important. By noon the sun would be out and he would be driving, and this time he would be in the brush down the stretch. During breakfast and even during his father's telephone call to the clinic, Gibson's mind was on the race.

Trudging up the forbidding stone steps of the clinic, Gibson was seized with a sudden desire to run away. He thought about the time when he was a small boy riding his

Shetland and they had come to a field where there was a big white object. At first it looked like a stone. Then the white thing began rolling and turned out to be a sow, and the pony had wheeled and bolted for home.

"What would you do," Gibson asked his father, smiling yet half serious, "if I turned tail and ran away?"

"Hang onto you, of course—the way you hung on when your pony saw the sow."

It was like that often. His father, it seemed, knew Gibson's very thoughts. Sometimes it worried him a little.

They walked into the white-walled waiting room and took the two end seats nearest the door. A woman, pencil and pad in hand, bustled up to them like a pacer in hobbles.

"Which of you is the patient?" she said in a voice that matched the starch of her uniform.

Mr. White said, "It's my son."

"Name and address?"

"Gibson White, at Ben White Stable, Lexington, Kentucky."

"Father's full name?"

"Benjamin Franklin White."

"Occupation?"

"Trainer of horses."

With a twitch of her nose as if she smelled something unpleasant, the woman turned on her heel and went back to her telephone and typewriter.

Now for Gibson came the uneasy time—the time of waiting, looking at old magazines, trying to read, but thinking instead. Thinking of the barns. There, the rain would not be dismal at all. It would thrum pleasantly on the stall roofs and drip in a beady curtain off the eaves, and the hay would smell sweet and the horses would be grinding it, glad of the day of peace.

Time strung itself out, as one after one the patients disappeared and new ones came to take their places. A fly drummed against the windowpane, getting nowhere. A child cried somewhere down the hall. At last the starched voice called out, "Dr. Mills will see you now, Mr. White."

Dr. Mills' office was as friendly as the reception room had been bleak. All over the wall were pictures of harness horses. And the man himself was friendly and big, overgrown like a Saint Bernard dog. His browned face looked to be on good terms with the wind and sun and rain. He picked up the card on his desk.

"The name Ben White is not new to me," he said, trying to remember. "Sit down, do. Oh, I have it now! Weren't you in the Hambletonian last year?"

"Yes, I drove one of Mr. Oliver's horses."

"Wasn't it a black by the name of Sonny Boy?"

"Laddy, it was," Mr. White smiled in answer. Then he gestured toward the Currier and Ives prints on the walls. He began naming the horses. "Dexter. Goldsmith Maid. Rysdyk's Hambletonian. Great names, those! You own a harness horse?"

"No, but I was born and raised in Orange County, New York, the cradle of the trotter. My hobby is harness racing. When I'm tired, nothing relaxes me like watching good trotters eat up the mile. Now, let's see." He looked at the card again. "Gibson White, patient? Say! you're not the cowboy that leaped aboard the runaway yesterday?"

Gibson laughed. Dr. Mills was a great guy. He knew horses!

"By Jove," the doctor chuckled, "I wanted to break through the crowd yesterday and meet this father-son team, and here they are! Now then, what brings you to me?"

He went back to his desk and picked up a pen that was tied by a long string to the holder. "Know why I do this?" he asked with a twinkle. "As a kid I had to have my mittens on a string so I wouldn't lose 'em. Now it's my pen."

He dipped it in an old-fashioned ink bottle and held the point poised over the card.

43

Mr. White's smile was gone. "It's Gib. He's been having too many colds."

Dr. Mills made an entry on the card. Then he sized up Gibson from head to foot. Growthy as any colt, he mused to himself. Turning to Mr. White, he asked, "Have you any work over at the stable on a rainy morning?"

"A trainer's work is like a woman's, Doctor. Never done."

"All right, then. Suppose you come back at noon. Meanwhile we'll go over this cowboy from forelock to boots."

They did go over Gibson, thoroughly. He champed and chafed under the ordeal. Why didn't they just give him some cough medicine the way veterinarians did for the horses? But no, he had to be shunted from one office to another, dressing and undressing, answering questions about himself, his mother, his father, grandparents on both sides.

Bald men, graying men, young men; brown eyes, blue eyes going over him as if he were a yearling for sale.

The only bright spot in the morning was the poem on one of the many walls he had to face. While a young doctor kept listening through his stethoscope, asking him to say "Ninety-nine, ninety-nine, ninety-nine," Gibson read the poem, sometimes missing a "ninety-nine."

If the poor victim needs must be percussed,
Don't make an anvil of his aching bust;
Doctors exist within a hundred miles
Who thump a thorax as they'd hammer piles;
So of your questions: don't in mercy try
To pump your patient absolutely dry;
He's not a mollusk squirming on a dish,
You're not Agassiz, and he's not a fish.
                              —OLIVER WENDELL HOLMES

44

When the doctor caught him reading the poem, the man and the boy exchanged a wink as if they had an enormous joke together.

The hands on the clock of the starched one's desk pointed to twelve when Mr. White, hat dripping rain, returned. He was ushered at once into Dr. Mills' office.

Gibson was already there, leaning forward in his chair, talking eagerly. "Yes, sir! We've got a great basketball team at U High," he was saying as Dr. Mills pulled a chair around for Mr. White.

"Play center, Gib?"

"Why, yes, I do!"

"And with those long legs I wager you're a track star, too."

"No," Gibson said. "Carroll Fisher has got me beat."

"Who's he?"

"He goes to U High with me."

"What's his record?"

"Eleven seconds in the hundred yard dash and twenty-three in the two hundred and twenty."

"What's yours?"

"Mine's eleven-three in the hundred, and twenty-four two in the two-twenty."

"I see. This Fisher chap is your competition."

Gibson leaned farther forward until he was on the very edge of his chair. "But I'm drilling hard," he said, "and I expect to improve. I like to box, too," he added.

Dr. Mills' sandy eyebrows went up. "Say, I used to be a pretty fair boxer in my day."

"When I was young," Gibson admitted, "I wanted to be the heavyweight champion of the world, but I've had to give up the idea."

45

"Why?"

"I'm too skinny."

"What about football, Gib?"

"Last season our school tied for first place."

"On the team?"

Gibson squirmed. "Just on the second team, sir."

"You play end?"

Gibson nodded, wide-eyed. "How did you know, sir?"

"Now what about your father's horses during the school year? When do you have time for them?"

"I had only a pony, but I used to jog him each morning before going to school."

"And after school there was either track or basketball or football?"

"Yes, sir."

"And of all these sports which do you prefer?"

Gibson did not hesitate. "Training and driving horses, sir. But I don't want to jog them forever. I want to compete in a real race. This afternoon's my first real one. We've got to be going, don't we, Dad?"

"I guess there's no hurry, Son. It's raining in earnest now."

Dr. Mills took off his glasses, folded the bows, and slid them into their case. He picked up his pen, then put it down again. He screwed the cap back on the ink bottle.

"Gibson!" he said, looking very hard at him, "what would you say if I owned a promising yearling and I asked you and your dad to develop him into a runner, a trotter, and a hunter?"

"You wouldn't ask it, sir."

"But suppose I did."

Gibson winked at his father. "I guess we'd just say we were too busy to take on any more horses, wouldn't we, Dad?"

46

"I guess we would, Son."

Dr. Mills and Mr. White exchanged glances.

"Why would you turn me down, Gib?"

"Because it wouldn't be fair to the horse."

The questions rained on. "Gib, what do you do when a horse has been over-trained?"

"We let up on him. Rest him a while."

"And if a horse has a cough and is off his feed?"

Gibson sat back in his chair. Fear spread suddenly over his face. "You're baiting a trap for me," he said with a hurt look, "and I'm . . ." his voice broke off, "I'm walking right into it."

There was a silence in the room. Gibson felt it around and about him, heavy and dense like fog. He was trying to grope his way out, trying to find a shaft of light. But there was none.

A voice penetrated the fog. It was Dr. Mills', and there was a tone of guilt in it as if he hated the words he had to say. "Gib, I once saw a colt worked until it began to weave with exhaustion. The trainer hadn't meant to overwork it. He thought the colt was ready. That sometimes happens, doesn't it, Ben?"

"Sometimes." Mr. White's face was grim and set. "Sometimes it does."

"What does the trainer do about it?"

Mr. White took a deep breath. He tried to make his voice sound matter of fact. "If it was a colt in my string, I'd see that he was sponged off and blanketed and bedded down in a good deep bed and then I'd let him sleep."

"Gib, between you and your dad you've written a good prescription. You've had a long workout. Now you've got to be unwound. Rest and the feed bag at regular intervals will do it." He pushed his chair back. "You know better than anyone else that it takes more than pluck to win a race. It takes endurance. We'll see that you get it." The doctor stood up now.

"And Gib," he added, "I know a hospital nestled in the Cumberland Mountains that will do for you what a green pasture will do for a colt."

Gibson choked out his next words. "How long? How long will I have to let up?"

"I don't know. Maybe only six months. Maybe longer."

There was a noise in Gibson's brain like the shattering of glass. It was louder than Dr. Mills' voice, louder than his father's. He couldn't hear what the voices were saying for the crashing sound. What did it matter what they said? Six months! It might as well be six years. Or sixty! The Grand Circuit was on! He was ready to drive! Six months! And then suddenly the noise in his brain stopped and there was that awful stillness that follows a crash.

He wanted to hide his head in his arm and sob like a kid. He might have done it, too, if only Dr. Mills had been there. But with his father he couldn't. "Thoroughbreds don't cry," his father would say as he used to say when a colt pulled up lame after a race. "They fight to get the lead again. Then they keep it."

Gibson stood up. He could feel his father's eyes on him. He took a hitch in his belt, trying to look as if nothing was happening to him.

Dr. Mills put his hand on the boy's shoulder. "Like to read, Gib?"

"Yes, sir," the voice was numbed and small.

"I'd prescribe that. And you can keep up with your school work. You'll probably get top grades now with all the time you'll have."

Six

Wɪᴛʜ all the time you'll have!" Time! From that hour in Dr. Mills' office the days and nights stretched themselves out beyond all believing. The sun dawdled and lazied in the sky like some giddyhead actor not knowing when to get off stage. When finally it slid behind the curtain of night, the green-cheese moon came out. The moon was even more of a dawdler than the sun! There were nights when Gibson longed to bend a giant hook and snag it out of the sky to hurry the time along.

Even his own clock had gone in league with the sun and the moon. At home in his room it had always been in a tearing hurry, hands flying. But here on the hospital dresser it piddled and pottered in maddening slowness—a *tick,* and a *tock,* and a *tick,* and a *tock.*

Gibson occupied a neat white bed in a sunny room, but

waking or sleeping he was back at the stable, his brown dog at his heels. He had only to close his eyes to make the whole scene come alive—horses flying around the track, the high shrill whinnies of the ones left behind. He felt left behind, too. He wanted to let out a great bellowing cry that would tear the stillness of the hospital into little shreds.

Everywhere, in everything, were reminders of the place where he belonged. By day hummingbirds visited a row of hollyhocks outside his window, and in the blur of their wings he saw the whirring of sulky wheels. At night, with head pillowed in his arms, he couldn't escape an incessant muffled beating—tap-tap, tap-tap, tap-tap, tap-tap. Hoofbeats? Or was it the mocking of his heart?

Dr. Mills paid fleeting visits, but they were disappointing. The talk balked and got nowhere. The doctor seemed more of a stranger than on that first day at the clinic. Not because he wasn't jovial and friendly; it was just that his laughter had a hollow sound.

Letters came but they, too, were sterilized of excitement. Never a word about things that mattered. About breeding and foaling and training and racing. No mention of the Big Apple. Or the Hambletonian. Or the Kentucky Futurity. No mention of horses or drivers. Not even of Bear. It was as if the whole world of stable and track had dropped into a sinkhole.

We're having Indian summer, the letters said. *Miss Briggs is sending your history book with each day's assignment marked. Our pear trees are loaded with fruit. We are shipping you a box of the Bartletts.*

The letters piled up. *We had our first frost. Grandmother is knitting you some nice warm bedsocks. Your English teacher is mailing you Shakespeare's play, "As You Like It."*

Bedsocks and Shakespeare! Soon he'd be letting his hair grow. Soon he'd turn into a sniveling sissy. He'd probably be knitting, himself!

And still more letters with all the marrow sucked out of them. *Snow today. We're proud of the marks you are getting this year. Even your father is noticing.*

Spring. *The hills are wild with redbud and dogwood. Your marks showed straight A's. We're proud of you, Son.*

Who wanted to read letters about marks and the weather! Who wouldn't get good marks when there was no football practice, no baseball, no basketball, no track, no horses to jog? Nothing to do but rest, rest, rest!

He would have thrown the whole batch of letters into the waste basket, except . . . Except for what? He didn't quite know. Maybe it was the handwriting. Maybe there was something in the writing that showed a holding back. Things unsaid. Maybe the hand wanted to write, *Out at Walnut Hall Alma Lee dropped a foal. A little stud colt. Small, but all horse.* It was about time, he knew. *We have twenty-five colts in training now. We're tuning up three for the Hambletonian. We could have taken on more colts, but you see, Gib, Dad is shorthanded. He needs you. Hear that, Gib? He needs you.*

But the letters were not like that. Only weather reports! That's all they were. Nothing but the weather. And in the boxes that came, only things to eat. Cookies. Apples. Pears. Food and more food, and no hunger to make you want it.

Then one morning Dr. Mills stood in the doorway and Gibson saw in a flash that some of the big-dog happiness had come back. "Gib!" he said, his eyes smiling, "your dad is on his way to Longwood and he's stopping off here. I'm going to meet him at the train. Now!"

The car wound up and up the mountains from the little station in the valley. The two men in the front seat hemmed and hawed and then drew into themselves. Dr. Mills sat huddled over the wheel, looking dead ahead. He had rehearsed everything he wanted to say, but now he had lost the key word.

"You're not satisfied with the boy's progress, are you?" Mr. White tried to make a beginning.

"That's it, Ben," Dr. Mills answered, "and I think I'm at fault."

Mr. White had nothing to say. He fingered his tie, loosened his collar as if his worry were choking him.

"The boy is like you, Ben. Like you and Tom Berry and all the others. There are only five letters in his alphabet. And they spell h - o - r - s - e."

The car labored up the mountain in low gear. "Hasn't he been working with you, Doc? Trying to get well?"

The doctor spoke as though to himself. "He's been trying so hard I can't look at him without . . ." He let the sentence peter out and started again. "A doctor begins to doubt himself when he has a patient like Gib."

"Is he eating, Doc?"

"He's trying to. But he chokes things down as if a lump in his throat left little room for food."

"I had a notion things weren't right." Mr. White ran the car window down to get all the air he could. "It's his letters. They don't sound like him. Never asks about how many horses are in training or who won the Kentucky Futurity or did Alma Lee have her colt. All he talks about is the weather. Who wants to know about the weather? With me, it's the weather in his mind that counts."

Dr. Mills nervously tapped the flat of his hand on the

steering wheel. "I was wrong in telling you not to write about your training problems. Gib's there with you, anyway. He might as well know how it really is. The good and the bad.

"Let's try out a new idea!" he added quickly, forcing a note of cheer into his voice. "Suppose, Ben, you face about and fill your letters with news, real news—breeding and training—actual problems. Send Gib clippings. Send his harness horse magazines. Make him feel he still belongs."

A great sigh of relief escaped Mr. White. "I'll do it, Doc! Fact of the matter is, I've wanted to all along." He thought a moment. "Yes, I'm sure the boy needs a strong dose of horse medicine. A stronger dose than can come in a letter."

"Horse medicine? Oh, well," Dr. Mills laughed a little wistfully, "there was a time I wanted to be a veterinarian, anyway. But seriously, Ben, what are you driving at?"

"Just this. One of the owners I train for gave me a high-strung filly by the name of Alma Lee."

"Yes?"

"And last year I bred her to the stallion Scotland."

"Yes, yes, go on."

"And day before yesterday, May fifth it was, she dropped a little brown foal." Now the words came out in a torrent. "And I've come to ask if you don't think this foal'd make a good dose of horse medicine for Gib. If I give her to Gib, I could train her for him and whatever he wanted done with her I'd do. No trainer would ever work harder to please an owner than I'd try to please him."

Dr. Mills blasted away on his horn. He pressed his foot on the accelerator even though they were going around a curve. "Why, that little tyke'll do more for the boy than fifty doctors," he crowed. "Great guns, what are we waiting for!"

Seven

GIBSON lay staring at the empty space between the windows when suddenly an old pork-pie hat came sailing into his room. Then a familiar figure strode joyously after it.

"Gib!" The father's eyes found the boy's, then wrenched away. There was a wild-bird look in them as if he'd broken a wing and now came flapping for help.

A quick hand thrust itself out from the covers. It was thin as any bird-claw, but Mr. White felt heartened a little by the firmness of its clasp. I've mended broken wings on birds and chicks, he thought, I can do it for my own. He picked up his hat and hung it on the chair, then sat on Gibson's bed.

Gibson sniffed. Ever so faintly the aroma of horse came to him. He sniffed again, smiling.

Mr. White took a long deep breath. "Shucks," he chuckled, "there's so much to tell you I hardly know where to begin. And we got to talk fast because I can't stay long."

"Busy, Dad?" asked Gibson, fighting his homesickness. "Lots of horses to train?"

"Busy!" Mr. White echoed. "So busy I was telling Guy only yesterday I'll be glad when you're ready to team in training with me."

Gibson's eyes looked full at his father. Behind the dark irises the yellow light searched him, pleading, thirsting, like shafts of sun reaching for water from the sea.

"It's the colts," Mr. White was saying. "Every time I see a little newborn I think of the flying potential in those long, slender legs."

They were quiet for a time, Mr. White not knowing how to go on. He walked over to the windows and looked out. "Pretty view," he said.

"Not bad," Gibson replied, "but too lonely. Needs some horses kicking up their heels."

Mr. White slapped his thigh. "By George!" He turned around, laughing. "It would be a sight fairer with a few brood mares and sucklings, chestnut and bay against the green."

He cleared his throat. "By the way, Gib, there's a . . ." He paused a second, then ventured, "There was a new foal born to Alma Lee just two days ago. I should be buckling a halter on it right now."

Horse talk! This was more like it! Gibson got out of bed, shuffled his feet into his slippers, and curled himself into the wing chair. He turned his face close to the old felt hat. "I'd been figuring it was about time, Dad." He took the hat in his hands, feeling of it. "A horse colt?"

"No. A filly."

"Is she little and fine like Alma Lee or big and rugged like Scotland?"

"My guess is she'll be big," Mr. White said. "Not coarse, you understand, just big-going like Scotland."

Excitement began to work into Gibson. He poked a finger under the crown of the hat and twirled it, the hat nodding and dipping as it spun. "With Alma Lee and Scotland for parents she ought to be something sharp."

"Yes. Royal ancestry."

Gibson felt good. This was almost like sitting out in front of the stables at dusk. All the work done. Just the talk, the soft-voiced talk. He let one arm dangle over the side of the chair, half expecting Bear's wet nose pushing into it, half hearing his tail thumping on the ground.

"You drove Scotland to his record, didn't you, Dad?" Gibson asked, trying to hold onto the moments.

Mr. White nodded. "A funny thing about him, Gib. That stallion'd never take dirt."

"You mean he'd always go around and never through the pack?"

"I do. Figure he saved my life once." Mr. White began remembering. "Scotland and I were in a race. A big one. And coming down the stretch one horse stumbled and fell and all those behind piled up in a heap. Tom Berry was one of the luckier ones. He got out with only a broken leg."

"And what about you, Dad?"

"Scotland traveled the big route and came on to win." Mr. White reached for the watch in his pocket.

Gibson rummaged in his mind for more questions. He couldn't let his father go. He wanted to hang onto him like a small boy grasping a coattail. "Who was Scotland's sire?" he asked quickly.

"He was Peter Scott. And he by Peter the Great." Mr. White began winding his watch.

"Did you know them?" Gibson hurried the questions, wanting to hear the answers but wanting more to string out the togetherness.

"I knew Peter Scott well," answered Mr. White. "A great friend of mine raced him—Thomas Murphy. That horse started in eighteen races and won seventeen."

Mr. White caught the ticking of the alarm clock and turned around to compare time.

"What about Alma Lee's side of the family?" Gibson blurted, then sighed in relief when he saw his father liked the question.

"I knew Alma Lee's father when he was just a little foal," Mr. White began fondly, rocking back and forth on his heels. "Drove him and his father, Lee Axworthy, too. He was the first two-minute trotting stallion in the whole world." The contented rocking and the words to match went on. "For my say-so, Lee Axworthy was the most wonderful horse ever looked through a bridle. From the time he was a three-year-old he broke from a trot only once, and that when another horse collided with him. And his son, Lee Worthy," Mr. White chuckled, "was something, too! When we'd score for the word 'Go' that horse'd look out the tail of his eye, wait for the other horses to come alongside, then *zzt*—he was off!"

Gibson's face was alert with interest. "I can remember when I was a little boy and picked some marigolds growing on his grave in the centerfield of the Lexington track."

Mr. White chuckled. "Your mother didn't think they were quite so pretty when she found out where you'd picked them. But I didn't come to talk pedigrees," he hurried on. "I'll tell you about just one more of the foal's ancestors and then I really must go. Volga, Alma Lee's granddam, was the world's champion filly. Never lost a race! Not one. And when you were a little knee-breech boy tutoring with Miss Branham, this Volga threw her into a tailspin."

"You mean Miss Branham actually drove Volga and got spilled?"

"No, no," laughed Mr. White. "This was the way of it. While she tutored, you used to hold the stop watch on her."

"Why, Dad, I didn't even own one."

" 'Course not. But you had a little old wrist watch and you made sure the lesson ended on time. One day, however, she was talking about the rivers of Russia and mentioned the Volga, and for the first time she had your whole attention. She figured it was a turning point and you were suddenly getting to like school. But when the lesson was over and she wanted to know why you were so attentive, do you know what you said?"

"No, what?"

" 'My father drives a horse by the name of Volga.' "

A knock on the door broke into the laughter, and a nurse came in bringing two glasses of orange juice. She offered one to Mr. White and put the other on Gibson's bedside table. She reached for the thermometer in a glass on the dresser, then changed her mind, straightened the pillows on the bed, and turned back the coverlet. Without saying a word, she moved her eyes from Gibson to the bed and back to Gibson again.

With a sigh, he hung the old hat on the wing of the chair

and climbed into bed. The nurse nodded and left the room.

Before her footsteps died away, Mr. White had emptied the glass of orange juice and waited while Gibson drank his. Then he came around to the foot of the bed, standing there, holding onto the rail. He wondered why he was so slow getting to the point. I act as if it were bad news instead of good, he told himself.

"Gib," he said, looking straight at the boy, "you've got to direct the training of Alma Lee's filly because"—his words were no longer slow and methodical—"because," he almost shouted, "she's yours!"

Suddenly the bed seemed narrower to Gibson than any sulky. He gripped the mattress, hanging onto it in dizzy insecurity. He felt ashamed at once, as if he had dropped the reins in a race and were clutching the sulky frame. He made his hands let go.

"A baby trotter to train!" his voice started low, then cracked like a girl's. "Oh, Dad!"

Mr. White looked at his watch in earnest, not because time mattered. It could have stood still for all he cared. But because he could not meet Gibson's look. "Before I go back, Gib," he said, clearing his throat, "I'd like to have you name your filly so I can have her registered."

Gibson laughed out. "Why, how can I name her without seeing her?"

"Hmm. Hadn't thought of that. Guess I'll have to see her for you. Let me think," Mr. White paced up and down in the little space between the bed and the windows. "She's red bay and her little switch tail is black and she wears white coronets on her right forefoot and her left hind."

"White coronets on alternate feet." Gibson's eyes were set

afar off, seeing the slender legs twinking through the grass. "When she trots, her white feet will be going in unison, won't they?"

"So they will!"

"How high does she stand, Dad?"

Mr. White closed his eyes to remember. He began measuring, placing his hand first at his bottom vest button, then up a little and a little more. "Her ears'd come about high as your heart, I'd say."

"That's it, Dad! That's it!"

Mr. White waited, not understanding.

"Don't you remember in Shakespeare's *As You Like It?*"

"Pshaw, Son. You know I'm not one to do a lot of reading. You tell me."

"Well, I forget just how it was, but I think Jaques was the one who said to Orlando, 'What stature is Rosalind?' and Orlando said, 'Just as high as my heart.' So what would you think if we named the new foal Rosalind?"

Mr. White's eyebrows went up. "Sounds highborn, like the filly she is. Anyhow, as trainer and not owner, I'd say Rosalind it is! And a good name. If I'm not mistaken, she'll have heart enough for anything."

The silence that followed had a nice sound. Mr. White's slow, even breathing. The whisper of footsteps in the hall. And outside the window a wren sputtering. Now there was no scrabbling around for things to say. Questions could be put as they came.

"Owners have to pay for board and training for their horses, don't they, Dad?"

"I've been thinking about that, Gib. And I have so much faith in a colt by Scotland out of Alma Lee that I'm willing to stand the cost of hay and oats until she's a two-year-old. Then she can begin earning and you can pay me from her earnings."

"Okay, Dad. I'll buy a notebook and enter all the costs in it, starting with her first halter and her registration fee, right on until she's entered in the Hambletonian."

"There's only one thing I have to ask, Son."

Gibson looked at his father and his eyes were all sunlight now. "Ask anything, Dad."

Mr. White grew almost bashful, but his eyes did not break away. "When I'm in a race," he said softly, "and I call on a colt for the supreme effort, he seldom fails me. You, Gib—?"

Gibson winked at his father. And suddenly the fevered look, the pleading-bird look, seemed gone. There was determination behind that wink and both Mr. White and his son knew it. They were in a conspiracy together.

Eight

NOW, for Gibson, Time acted reasonable and right-minded again. The sun and the moon settled back into their old routine, traveling their orbits with business and dispatch. And the round-faced clock on the dresser ticked and tocked with dignified decorum.

Scarcely had Mr. White closed the door behind him than Gibson had something important to do. He suddenly remembered you couldn't name a colt just any name that occurred to you. It had to have a certain number of letters in it. So he wrote to the American Trotting Association, special delivery air mail, asking for the rules and regulations. Then he wrote his father, telling him not to apply for the certificate until he heard.

But in his own mind he would always call her Rosalind. There was no changing a name once it fitted.

The very same day of Mr. White's visit, Gibson ordered a black notebook from the hospital commissary and spent nearly all of one month's allowance for a fountain pen. This record of his filly had to be permanent. His first entry read: *Rosalind (temporary name) foaled May 5th, by Scotland out of Alma Lee. Color, bright bay. Markings, two white coronets. Trainer, Benjamin Franklin White. Owner, Gibson White.*

Then he began listing the items his father would need:

1 halter

1 lead strap

No hay yet

No straw

Foal is still sharing mare's stall. Eating off her.

Sleep was a long time coming that night of May seventh. When it did come, a big-going filly ran away with Gibson's dreams. She had wings growing out of her withers and she took off over fences and cliffs and mountaintops; yet, no matter how high her leap, she never broke from her trot. Gibson woke with a flash of joy over her way of going.

One morning a week later, Dr. Mills came again to see Gibson. Over his arm he carried two saddlebags. "These," he said with a show of pride, "belonged to my great-grandfather Samuel Mills. I spent nearly all of last night saddle-soaping them and splicing a piece onto the strap that joins them."

He came over to show Gibson. "See what a good job I did. Now whisk out of bed," he directed. "I've made the strap long enough to throw across your bedspring. Now you'll have one saddlebag at your right hand and one at your left—one for incoming mail, one for outgoing."

Gibson was out of bed, helping Dr. Mills lay the strap flat under his mattress, helping tuck the sheets back in place. He felt of the smooth leather, wishing he could sling the bags over Rosalind and trot around the Big Apple with just oats and a clean shirt in the pouches. But aloud he said, "Mail's going to be *worth* saving now."

"I've got another surprise, too." Dr. Mills started for the door. In a moment he was back again, this time carrying a big bulletin board. With hammer and nails from his pocket he hung it opposite the bed in the space between the windows.

"This won't be vacant long," he said, standing off and eyeing it with approval. "Here are some thumbtacks. I'll lay them beside your clock on the dresser. Whenever you have a picture or a clipping you want to hang on your bulletin board, you can get out of bed and do it yourself."

A sudden smile wreathed Gibson's face. "Isn't it—isn't it good, that of all doctors we found you!"

Dr. Mills looked pleased. He stood with hands in pockets, glancing from the bulletin board to the mail pouches and back again. "I'm going home to Orange County tomorrow," he said, "and the first free minute I have I'll rummage around in my attic there. I think I've a book about a great American trotter you'll like. Especially," his voice rolled out strong, "now you're an owner."

When Dr. Mills left, Gibson plunged his hands into the pockets of the saddlebags. They were good and deep, deep enough for whole packets of letters. Books, too.

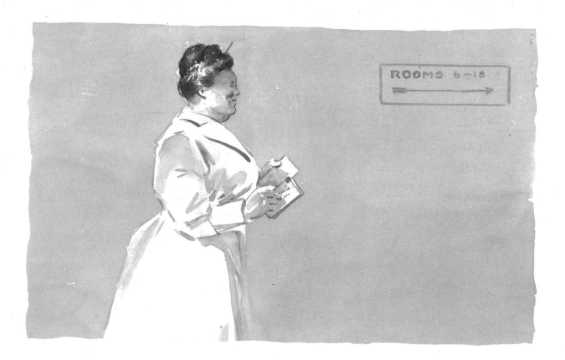

ROOMS 6-18

Nine

THE saddlebags were not long empty. At noon that day plump Miss Kierksted, whom everyone called Tante, came in waving two pieces of mail. "A letter for you, Gibchen, and the other looks like a picture." She smiled, showing little white teeth that reminded Gibson of a pet mouse he once had. "My, my!" she exclaimed, inspecting the new saddlebags, "aren't we fancied up! If my mail gets any heavier, I'll come in to borrow your pouches."

The minute the door closed, Gibson ripped open the bigger envelope. A slow grin spread over his face as he took out a tinted photograph of his father holding Rosalind in his arms as if she were a pup instead of a foal. And beside them stood Bear, looking up so lifelike Gibson half expected a yelp of joy. He studied the picture a long time, first at close range, then at arm's length, excitement growing within him. He rang for a nurse. Rosalind was too good to keep to himself. He had to spread the news. How curious yet trusting she was! How sure of her place in the world! How big-eyed!

"Gibson White! Answer me!" a laughing voice said. "I've been standing here two minutes."

Gibson looked up from his trance, then smiled in embarrassment. He handed the picture to the young nurse. "I just wanted you to see a picture of my new filly."

When he let the picture go, he saw it even more clearly. The up-headed little colt with the switch tail no longer than a whisk broom. The peppery look about her. And the deep pride in his father's face. He wondered if Alma Lee were half as proud of her foal as he was.

"Isn't she tiny!" the nurse exclaimed.

Gibson laughed aloud. "Why, she's going to be big and husky. She'll be sixteen hands when she's full grown."

"Hands?"

The boy nodded. "Four inches to a hand," he explained. "That means she'll probably be five feet and four inches over the withers when she's grown." He was pleased at the look of surprise the nurse gave him.

When she left, Gibson propped the picture on his knees and turned to the letter. It was in his father's handwriting, a whole page long and not a word about the weather!

Your filly, it began, *is nosy as any cat. I turned her and Alma Lee out to pasture today with a dozen brood mares and their foals. She had to snuff and snort to each of them. Her dam was in a dither. She knows a newcomer is an outcast for days and is usually greeted with flying heels and bared teeth.*

I wish you could have watched them. Your mother and I

decided Alma Lee would have made a good roundup pony. She'd nip her youngster very gently on the rump, then run her in ever-widening circles until finally she'd herded her away from the big mares.

Your Rosalind is full of ginger, you bet. Wild and uncertain as a deer. She bunts the daisies with her nose and nicks the clouds with her heels. And when she's through with her antics, she wades in that old frog pond down by the clump of willows. Sometimes she just stands there, admiring the little ripples around her feet.

By George, Son, this is the longest letter I've ever written an owner. I've got work to do! Good-by for now.—Dad

Gibson tacked the picture on the bulletin board. It was no bigger than a square of toast, but when he squinched his eyes it grew until the whole wall became a pasture with daisies in it, and Rosalind was snorting at them with her nose and beheading them with her heels, frisking and capering from one end of the pasture to the other. But what pleased Gibson most was that in her frisking she had no gallopy gait. It was all trot with her!

Then he opened his eyes and watched the picture shrink back to size. He laughed out at his wishfulness.

Ten

THE folks at the Trotting Association were prompt in answering letters. Gibson had a postcard from them in the same mail with the book from Dr. Mills.

Dear Sir: the neatly typed postcard read, *In answer to your letter, please be advised that names proposed for registration in the American Trotting Register shall be limited to sixteen (16) letters.*

Gibson counted on his fingers. R-O-S-A-L-I-N-D. Only eight letters! He was safe! At home he would have sounded out with an ear-splitting war whoop. But here he could only scribble the good news in handwriting that rocked wildly from margin to margin. He dropped the note to his father in the outgoing mail pouch. Then he slipped out of bed and tacked the card from the Trotting Association on his bulletin board. He liked the official look of it; it would do until the big certificate came.

As long as he was up, he decided to sample the day. He stood a moment looking out his window, his hands resting on the sill. Below him a wide expanse of well-tended lawn swept down to a mountain stream, and beyond the stream spruce-covered hills climbed up and up into the mist. Gibson noted again the untracked emptiness of the lawn. There was no motion anywhere. None at all. And the clear stream, too, seemed lonely, with no creatures mirrored in it.

Quickly he began stocking the scene with brood mares and foals. They were everywhere! Cropping the grass. Rolling in it. Pawing it. Plunging their muzzles in the stream. Plashing in it, sending up rainbows of spray. And one baby trotter with alternating white feet was headed toward him, her saucy tail outflung on the wind.

"A sight fairer!" he laughed as he crawled back into bed, sitting by mistake on the package with the book in it. He pulled it out from under him, examining the scrawly hand. *From Dr. S. W. Mills,* it said, *to Mr. Gibson White, Horseman.*

Gibson began to tear the wrappings as if he were opening just any package. But suddenly he caught sight of a gold hasp with a tiny padlock and key, and he saw the red binding frayed bare at the corners. His fingers slowed. This was not just any book. This book had been smoothed by many hands and many years, until it had the gloss of old feed boxes, satined by the tongues of many horses. Gibson ran a finger over the gold stamping—over the slim-bodied horse, over the spider-web wheels of the wagon, over the bearded man holding the reins, over the dates underneath the medallion, 1849-1876. He broke out in goose flesh as if he were putting a finger on the past and by so doing could make it come alive again. Aloud, he read out the title bannered in gold letters across the book.

Now he could wait no longer. With eager fingers he unlocked the hasp, then opened the cover as if it were made of glass. Carefully he began riffling the pages. They were yellowed darkly around the edges and had a brittle feel.

He skipped the preliminary pages and plunged into the story. And in the very first sentence he was lost. Lost in a broad valley with the wind blowing clean.

1: Sky-Borne

Feet planted wide in the peaty earth, William Rysdyk straightened from his ditching, rolled up his sleeves, took out a red bandanna handkerchief, and swabbed his sweating forehead and neck.

A rugged, muscle-powered man he was, and now he flexed and stretched and rose up on tiptoe like some Atlas propping the heavens with the pillars of his arms. Scraggly brows shadowed his deep blue eyes, and a full black beard grew down to hide the first two buttons of his linsey-woolsey shirt. His ears, rather large, were pointed a little at the top to give him the look of a leprechaun.

As he returned the handkerchief to its pocket, he jutted his beard to the sky. What he saw held him transfixed.

Appearing from nowhere at all, a cloud, massive and dark, loomed over Sugar Loaf Mountain, then in one motion scudded up to the sun and inked it out. William Rysdyk stood aghast.

The cloud was clean-formed, and its likeness was a stallion— a stallion that stood wide on the sky. He was veined with light, his mane was on end in licks of flame, his upflung tail was fringed with fire, and his nostrils blew sparks so that the sky was all horse and the valley all his shadow.

'Ai yai yai!' breathed William Rysdyk above the tremor in his throat. 'Yonder he is, himself! *Who else?*'

So lost was he in the spectacle that the voice of his employer fell on him like a weight.

'Rysdyk! Rysdyk!'

Startled, the hired man came back to himself. He looked over his shoulder to see handsome Jonas Seely astride his gray gelding.

'Excuse, sir?' William Rysdyk asked, puckering his lips as if he were saying O.

Mister Seely's voice filled the valley, then the mountain took it up and buffeted the sound back. 'Rysdyk! June is blowing across the land!'

What kind of talk was this! How could a month go blowing? The hired man stood with questioning eyes, watching Mister Seely gesture toward the upland pasture.

'The steers are sleek and stout,' he pronounced, 'and the gloss on the Alderney bull is high. Friday next, if Mister Townsend can spare you, we will drive them to New York market.'

The hired man nodded absently, as if going to market were no adventure at all.

'And I have also come to make a survey of your progress with the drainage ditch. Lay a footbridge across about here,' Mister Seely directed, 'about where Sir Luddy's forefeet stand.'

'Yah, sir.' The answer was a faraway singsong as William Rysdyk's gaze was drawn back to the sky. The horse-cloud still blotted the sun, but the animal's spirit was gone. The fire had died, leaving a dim, vaporous creature in its place.

'Rysdyk!' There was irritation in Mister Seely's voice. It made his face red and his muttonchop whiskers very white. 'What holds you in a trance? What is it?'

A work-soiled finger pointed to the sky. Mister Seely looked, and even without the fiery spirit the phenomenon cast its spell over him. He tied the reins in a knot and leaned back, his hands on Sir Luddy's hips. ' 'Tis strange,' he exclaimed, 'how man can witch the clouds. I see in them a ghost mare.'

'You too, sir?' The question had a note of admiration in it.

'Aye,' Mister Seely breathed quickly. 'The cloud is a ghost from my boyhood.'

Now that his stallion had faded, William Rysdyk looked up no more. He bent to his ditching, then thought better of it. Maybe, he said to himself, if I listen sharp and nice to Mister Seely's remembrances, then maybe Mister Seely to me listens. 'How was she called, sir?' he asked, but not really caring.

Mister Seely's eyes were fixed on the cloud. 'She was called Silvertail because of a tuft of silver hair at the root of her tail.'

'And does it yet grieve you for her?'

'No, no! Not now,' chuckled Mister Seely. 'That was nigh onto forty years ago.'

'A year already before I was born.' The questions stopped. Try as he would, William Rysdyk could not keep his mind on Mister Seely's ghost mare. He returned to his work, digging and pitching, pitching and digging.

'What, Rysdyk?'

'I didn't say nothing.'

But Mr. Seely could not wait for questions. He was bursting with memories. 'I'm minded of the time Silvertail galloped seventy-five miles in a day.' He glanced down quickly at his hired hand for an 'Ai yai yai.' When none came, he went on. 'And my

75

father and I were riding double to boot! Of course, I was a mere sprout of a boy at the time. Ten or thereabouts.'

'By golly,' said William Rysdyk with no emphasis at all.

'Aye. There was a mare! She came by her spirit honestly. Her sire was the Imported Messenger, brought over from England.'

At the word 'Messenger' William Rysdyk's head jerked up, his beard parting in the little wind. This was a name he knew! 'Sir! A question I could want to ask.'

'Ask!' encouraged Mister Seely.

'When Messenger stomps down the gangplank, what they say about him—it is true?'

'Indeed so. When his boat landed at Philadelphia, the other horses were too weak to walk down the gangplank—'

'And him, sir?'

'He came charging down, lifting two grooms off their feet, up and down like pump handles. Then he ran through the streets of Philadelphia, the grooms dangling along like birds on a string.'

William Rysdyk laughed, wishing he had been there to see.

'Silvertail was like him!' Mister Seely said proudly. Suddenly he was embarrased by all this talk of himself and his mare. He turned kindly to his hired man. 'Did you ever see a horse that fastened itself on your memory?'

William Rysdyk stood helpless. He felt dumb, like the steers with their wet noses and their big stand-out ears. He looked around awkwardly, letting the gelding lick the salt of his hand. 'My words, sir, lie all together in a heap.' He glanced up to the cloud. And wonder of wonders, the stallion was on fire again, high-tailing for the mountain, leaving streaks of flame across the sky.

'Mister Seely!' he yelled in excitement. The words usually so slow in forming tumbled out in a rush. 'Once some water I was pumping up and a horse and rider go by me. And I forget to pump up only one of my buckets. I forget I must home. My mother the evening meal is making ready. I just stand. The horse—in his eye a look he had. How is called that in the English?'

'The look of eagles?'

'Yah, yah! The eagle look he had.' William Rysdyk's head nodded excitedly, the chords in his neck swelling. 'Now comes it, sir!' His voice hushed. 'Now comes the best part. The evening is pulling down already. But the rider turns the horse and they make for me. And they stop. And I water the horse from our own drinking pail. He drinks it all, with the eagle look still looking.'

William Rysdyk was trembling violently. 'And when he gallops away, I just stand. Yah,' he nodded, 'I just stand until the mama calls. And she yells, "Will-yum! Pump out!" And I to her yell, "There comes no water out!" And she yells, "Pump! You not pumping!"'

Now it was William Rysdyk's turn to be embarrassed. He looked down at his big hands. 'You think I stay just at the talking?' he asked. 'I must hurry myself along with the ditching. No?'

'Not yet, Rysdyk. I find myself curious as to the stallion's name. Do you know it?'

A deep guttural laugh accompanied the answer. 'To my first memory belongs the name. It stabs like a dagger in my head. Hamble-tonian it was, called after Hambleton, a race course in England. The man, he was called by the name Bishop. And the horse, he was the son of Messenger.'

Mister Seely was out of the saddle, grasping William Rysdyk, shaking him until the hairs in his black beard jumped up and down like wire springs. 'Bishop's Hambletonian!' he thundered. 'Egad, Rysdyk, my father bred Silvertail to your stallion!'

And overhead the cloud wisped off into nothing and the brassy sun came out.

77

Eleven

WITH his finger marking the picture, Gibson looked up a moment at his bulletin board as if to make sure of Rosalind. Satisfied, he let the book fall open again. He was going to like it! That man Rysdyk was a character! Tough and strong as a bull. Gibson didn't quite see what the strange cloud shape had to do with the great American trotter, but he liked the story anyway.

His eyes caught the stack of textbooks on his table, their bookmarks pointing accusing fingers at him. He turned away quickly. Studies could wait. He glanced at the round-faced clock and it seemed to be winking, in league with him now.

I'll read just another page or two, he thought. And the clock ticked, "Why not? Why not?"

He peeked at the title of the next chapter and with that he was swept into the past.

2: Butcher's Nag

William Rysdyk forgot the cloud image in his first trip to New York City. To him the journey was good beyond all dreaming. The teamwork between Mister Seely and himself was so nice and precise. They were a matched pair! That Mister Seely, he thought, is not afraid of the work. Here, there, everywhere he is. Herding the cattle out of the brush, away from grazing space, around a hill, keeping them always on the go.

'Boss good!' he kept chuckling to himself, proud of his employer. 'Like he was born with a horse under him, he rides.'

He had no idea that Jonas Seely was equally proud of his hired man. Here was a drover, Mister Seely thought, who prodded the steers with his voice. Not his stick.

Along the way whole families came running when they saw the cloud of dust rising as the cattle clumped toward them. Out of their fields and kitchens they came, waving broad hats and sunbonnets, shooing the steers, keeping them from turning into the farm lanes and joining their own cattle.

Sometimes they were round-faced Dutch folk who stood in shy embarrassment when pompous Mister Seely rode up. But when they heard the familiar singsong of William Rysdyk's speech, they invited him and Mister Seely too into their snug, whitewashed houses.

'Come,' they would urge, 'is nooning time. Our Hans and Hendrick the cattle for you can watch. The eating is ready. It gives runderslappen and fresh crullers.'

Such good food it was! Even Mister Seely, used to porridge

and cold mutton at noon, passed his plate for second helpings of runderslappen, the thick-sliced beef spiced with apples and cloves. Often there was lentil soup, too, made with pigs' feet and sausage, and for dessert a huge bowl of crullers, filled from a bottomless crock.

And so the employer on horseback and the drover afoot made a pleasant junket of the journey southward along the Hudson River until they approached New York.

Once in the hurry-scurry of the city, however, William Rysdyk was a man lost. The city sounds boxed his ears and bewildered his

mind. By day he felt himself a frighted hound, hugging his master's heels. By night in his bed in the Bull's Head Tavern, the city vehicles and the river craft seemed to rumble over his very body. He could hardly breathe for the hurting of the noise.

Afterward, he remembered very little of the city itself. He recalled, as in a dream, the livestock parade with bands playing and bells ringing and people's heads sprouting out of windows. And he remembered he was in the parade, holding the lead shank of the Alderney bull. But of the sea of people on either side of him he remembered not one face. Of Pearl Street and Wall Street and Broadway he could recall not one building. Of the awarding of a silver trophy to Mister Seely he remembered only that the sun glanced off it, almost blinding him. The words said he could not remember. They were mere puffs of smoke.

But with the parade over and the cattle sold and now the joyous prospect of going home, everything suddenly came sharp and clear. William Rysdyk was in the box of the cart, alone now that the prize bull had been sold at auction. And Mister Seely, sitting on the driver's seat beside Butcher Kent, was holding the trophy his Alderney had won.

'I'll drop you and your man at the Bull's Head,' Mister Kent was saying. 'You know, of course, that you are expected at the turtle feast of the Agricultural Society this evening. It is my duty to arrange the seating of the dignitaries.'

Mister Kent looked for and got no answer, for he was making a great flourish with his whip. And the rough-coated mare that drew the cart was taking off at a good gait, picking her way through the streets in elegant style. Dogs and cats and a big fat goose retreated in alarm.

'For an old mare,' Mister Seely said loudly, leaning forward in pleasure, 'she is quick and trappy.'

Mister Kent nodded. 'Aye!' he shouted, 'and she should be! I got her of a banker who paid six hundred dollars for her. Under saddle she twice trotted the Union Course at a two-fifty clip.'

'Eh?' grunted Mister Seely in astonishment.

William Rysdyk held onto the sides of the cart, spraddling his feet to steady himself as they lunged and lurched over the rough streets.

'And where did the banker get her?'

'From a fish peddler who'd paid out a paltry sum for her.'

Mister Seely's next words jerked out to the motion of the cart. 'There's something about her head . . . and her way of going . . . and the angling of her hock . . .' But the wind scattered his words.

'The banker,' Mister Kent offered, 'gave me no papers with her. Nor a name. We call her Butcher's Nag from her habit of pulling up lame after a day's work.'

As if the mare had overheard, she began limping, and by the time they reached the Bull's Head Tavern she was a pitiable sight with her uneven gait.

William Rysdyk jumped out of the cart, waiting for Mister Seely, but his employer was deep in thought.

'What of her lameness?' he asked, looking at Mr. Kent.

'I know not the particulars.' The man's eyes glinted as he slowly returned the whip to its socket, sensing a deal in the air. 'I was told there was an accident,' he replied, measuring his words. 'The mare had good cause to shy and run away, and the chaise swung into a tree. As I heard it, she got her leg caught in one of the wheels and she herself was thrown to the paving stones.'

'The result a spavin?'

'A slight one,' nodded Mister Kent, forgetting about the seating of the dignitaries. 'Only when she is tired would you observe it.'

'I find it somewhat of a smart,' Mister Seely said, plucking at the tufts of his muttonchop whiskers, 'to see a mare put to work with a bad spavin.'

'The spavin is nothing, I tell you. In the morning, rested, she will go sound.'

The question Mister Kent looked for came more quickly than he expected. 'What will you take for your Butcher's Nag?' Mister Seely inquired.

From the stables beyond the inn, two grooms came up, listening, awaiting orders.

'Go on about your business,' Mister Kent told them not un-kindly. Then turning to Mister Seely, 'I'll take a hundred and thirty-five for her.'

Looking at the mare, William Rysdyk swallowed. A hundred and thirty-five taler! Why, she was over the fifteen. Over the twenty, maybe.

'It is too steep a price,' Mister Seely was saying without any rise in his voice. 'You know it full well. And I know it.'

'P'raps so. P'raps so. But I too bought her with the same spavin. And, I might add, at the same figure. Now I really must be off.'

Mister Seely got down from the cart, thinking. 'The turtle feast tempts me,' he said, yawning, 'but I believe I will rest against the morrow's journey.' He lowered his voice. 'Should the mare go sound by noontide, I will buy her at your price. She might make a good brood mare.'

The two men shook hands to seal the agreement. Then William Rysdyk and Mister Seely stood watching as the mare limped away, until she and her cart were swallowed by the lengthening shadows.

Twelve

GIBSON was brought back to the here and now by a sharp pinch of his toe.

"That book must be something!" A nurse stood laughing at the foot of the bed, holding a tray on her arm. "Your lunch is getting cold." She turned and set the tray down on a small table beside the wing chair. "You can get up to eat it," she said, opening out the drop leaf. "And Tante has put your mail on the table. She felt put out that you didn't even know she was here."

For the first time since he had left the Grand Circuit, Gibson was hungry. With each mouthful of meat loaf and tomato sauce he made believe he was eating runderslappen smothered in spicy gravy. And the gingersnaps on his tray were not gingersnaps at all; they were rich, crumbly crullers.

Chewing his food, he slit open the letter with his forefinger. He read it not once, but two and three times over.

Your filly's got horse sense, Son. No bees in her bonnet. Knows enough to take a good snooze in the afternoon, lying down.

The other day I was showing her to Mr. Reynolds and Bill Strang and she dropped into a trot and strode off with fine knee action. By George, they were impressed. I was puffed up as a bullfrog over it.

Gibson laughed, took another mouthful, read on.

The fast trot is becoming a habit with her. She's the first one to reach the gate at feeding time and she always comes on a trot.

Gibson poured himself a glass of milk from the pitcher on his tray.

Dr. Mills found a cabin near the hospital for your mother and grandmother. You can expect them for a visit any day now.

I'm sending you a catalog of training gear so you'll know costs.

Gibson emptied his glass of milk and glanced through the catalog. "Gosh," he said, "Rosalind's going to have to be a two-minute horse to pay her keep!" Two minutes! He took hold of the cords on his bathrobe. He closed his eyes. The cords became reins and the pull on them was strong, and Rosalind was flying down the stretch. He could hear the sound of her hoofs on the track. She could do it! The two-minute mile was a breeze.

Each letter about his filly seemed to bring new strength to Gibson. And some days the hands on the clock flew around in a tearing hurry, exactly as they had done on his dresser at home. There was so much to do! Rosalind's progress to be entered in the notebook. Lessons to be worked out and sent back to school. Letters to be written. And each day his mother and grandmother came, remembering important things.

"Bear naps right between Rosalind's feet. And she stands quiet and gentle, not daring to move until he wakes,"—this was his grandmother speaking.

"Rosalind's tail beckons when she goes," his mother said.

The talk had stuff and purpose. No little surface words like "Everything's fine. Isn't the weather lovely?"

But it was strange how Gibson lived in two worlds now. Part of the time he was himself, Gibson White, owner of Rosalind in training for the Grand Circuit. And part of the time he was a rugged hired hand, strong as all outdoors. The big black beard didn't make William Rysdyk a character remote at all. It was like a Hallowe'en mask. Behind the beard Gibson saw an overgrown boy. At home under the sky. Boxed in and wretched in the city

The moment visiting hours were over, Gibson crawled back into his other world. Even when famous baseball players came to the hospital and looked in on him, their good-bys still echoed while his hands were reaching out for the book, finding the place.

3: A Bargain Made

Precisely at the hour of noon, Mister Kent appeared at the Bull's Head Tavern with the mare tied to the tail of a wagon.

'Here she is! And sound as a dollar,' he announced to Mister Seely as he untied her and walked her about. 'Note,' he said, 'how the swelling has subsided and the lameness with it.'

Mister Seely tilted his head, watching to see if the mare placed her weight evenly on all four feet. 'Hmm,' he mused in unbelief, for her feet touched the ground smartly, each stroke quick and strong.

William Rysdyk stared in astonishment as he saw ten- and twenty-dollar gold pieces go from Mister Seely's pocket into the cupped hands of Mister Kent. And, dumbfounded, he heard the calm words, 'Here are the gold pieces you paid out for the Alderney; your own dollars come back to roost!'

On the way out of the city, Mister Seely rode Sir Luddy and William Rysdyk led the mare. It was true about her going sound after a night's rest. She raised her knee and hock well, thrusting her legs forward and backward in a smooth stroke.

Not a word passed between the two men until they had crossed King's Bridge over the Spuyten Duyvil Creek and were out on the Harlem Valley Road.

Then Mister Seely made an eyeshield of his hand. He looked ahead and he looked behind. 'Whoa, Rysdyk!' he commanded when he had made certain no one was anywhere in sight. 'Now look! Does the butcher's nag have a star? Very small? High under the forelock?'

Quick hands lifted the graying lock of hair. 'Yah, shure.'

'And is one foreleg more roan than bay?'

'Shure, shure. Already I see it in New York.'

'Look sharp! Does she have a fine white coronet on her near, no, on her off hind leg?'

William Rysdyk walked around and observed. 'Yah, on her off side, sir, if you look hard.'

The questions streamed on. 'Look, Rysdyk! On the neck under her mane. A quirl?'

'How say you?'

'A quirl—a spot where the hair grows frowardly?'

William Rysdyk lifted the mane. And there, underneath, just as Mister Seely had said, was a little spot where the hair grew wayward. 'Shure! Shure! The hairs they turn themselves around!'

Mister Seely threw back his head and slapped his thigh. 'It's the same mare all right,' he chuckled, as if enjoying some secret joke. 'The same mare brother Peter rode. She could be a vixen, Rysdyk, if it were not for that bad spavin.'

'Yah?'

'Now leg up on her. You're not so old as your beard makes you out. I wager she'll feel younger as she gets to traveling country roads instead of cobblestones. Here, lead her alongside. That's it. Now put your foot in my stirrup and leap aboard. No need of a bit and bridle. She'll stay close to Sir Luddy for companionship.'

William Rysdyk vaulted onto the mare's back and snugged his knees into place. He felt her alert. And all of a sudden he was elevated in spirit as well as body. 'Ach!' he cried in ecstasy. 'I feel myself big. Look once, sir. By golly, she stands me good! You think maybe I fit her all right?'

Mister Seely's nod left no doubt.

For the first time in his life William Rysdyk was riding alongside Mister Seely. For the first time he was astride a fine trappy animal instead of a broad-backed work horse. As they journeyed along he could not help comparing the mare with Sir Luddy. 'That Luddy, he is jughead alongside her,' he said to himself. 'By criminy, with her rough coat yet she's beautiful like anything.'

They rode on in silence, following the silver river, going slowly along like the steamboat lazing downstream.

At last Mister Seely broke into the quiet. 'This mare without a name,' he said as they ambled along, 'is a great-granddaughter of Messenger.'

'So? That explains it why she could go around the Union Course so quick?'

'That is but part of the reason.'

'Yah?'

'Yes, but a part.'

A flock of wild pigeons flew low over their heads, the noise of their wings shutting out the talk.

'How you going to say, sir?' reminded William Rysdyk when the whistle of bird wings had gone by.

Jonas Seely laughed loud and long until the blood deepened in his face. It made his white stock look whiter than the underside of the pigeons. Could be a stroke striking him! the hired man thought in alarm. Then he sighed with relief as Mister Seely went on.

'The mare you ride,' he chortled, 'had no time to wait for a name. She was a runaway at every chance.' His laughter broke out afresh. 'One day my brother limped home from a ride and sold her off quick as scat before his bruises had a chance to heal.'

'Yah?' asked William Rysdyk, his eyebrows crawling up and up his forehead.

'The wings on her heels came from—'

'Yah? Yah?'

'They came from her grandsire and granddam.' Mister Seely slapped a fly that worried his horse.

William Rysdyk could stand the suspense no longer. Now his face was red, too. 'And who *was* they, sir?' he exploded.

'They were,' said Jonas Seely, stretching out the words until they snapped into the hired man's face, 'they were my Silvertail and your Bishop's Hambletonian.'

A gasp came from the black beard. 'Bishop's Hamble-tonian!' The hands holding the halter rope began to shake and the bronzed face went ashy gray. With a little cry no more than a dog's whimper, William Rysdyk toppled from the mare's back into the dust of the road.

Like a scalded cat she bolted up the pike, the lead rope snaking out behind her.

Thirteen

GIBSON thought he heard a knocking. He swung around to listen. There! It came again. Louder.

He raised himself on both elbows. "Come in," he said, trying to hide the annoyance he felt.

A tall, dark-eyed woman entered his room carrying a basket on her arm. The basket was filled with books in yellow and red and green jackets.

"Good morning," she said, stopping just inside the door. "Would you like to select a book from our new library? A mystery? A western? A sea story, perhaps?

Gibson found it difficult to wrench his mind away from the book in his hands. What was happening to the runaway mare? Would she ever race again? Would she get worse and be led away to her death? "No, thank you," he managed to say politely, "I have a book, and schoolwork, too."

A hurt look came into the woman's eyes. She turned to leave, the heavy basket sagging her shoulder.

"Wait," Gibson called, feeling mean. "I could see what you have, and when you come next time . . . ."

She came back, smiling, resting the basket on the edge of his bed. "May I look at your book while you look over these?"

Gibson gave her the old, old book while he glanced at the titles in her basket. *Smoky,* by Will James. *Twenty Thousand Leagues under the Sea. Death at Dawn.* And tucked in between *Adventures of Tom Sawyer* and *Mutiny on the Bounty* was a book on boxing. "I'd like this one," he said, pointing to it. "Could you bring it next time you come?"

The woman nodded, wrote down the book title on a scrap of paper, picked up her basket and was gone. But before Gibson could go back to his reading, the door opened again and his mother came in. She read aloud a letter from Miss Briggs, asking why she had not received his mathematics paper.

"I'll just stay and wait while you do it," Mrs. White said, taking out her knitting and making herself comfortable in the wing chair.

Gibson sighed as he opened the textbook and found the problems he was to solve. How many rolls it took to paper Mr. Anderson's circular room, nine feet high, diameter twelve feet, seemed small doings while a lame mare was streaking off, unguided, over dangerous terrain. Each problem was more irksome than the one before. The same Mr. Anderson was offered as many flagstones as he wanted at two cents a stone. And the question was how many would he need and how many pounds would they weigh and how much would it cost to build a terrace of such and such dimensions. There were twelve problems, all about this Mr. Anderson and his busyness. Gibson fairly hated the man by the time they were worked out and given to his mother to mail.

It was night before he found time to read. No sound anywhere except the distant cry of a screech owl. He sighed in anticipation. His supper tray had been picked up. The room straightened. Evening visitors gone. A whole hour before lights would go out. And now, at last!

His hands went to the table beside his bed. He lifted the harness horse magazines. He lifted some old newspapers. But the book with the gold hasp was not there.

He felt in his mail pouches, in the outgoing and the incoming. It was not there, either.

He pawed through the things in his dresser, knowing all the while the book could not possibly be there. He looked underneath the bed. There was nothing. Only his shadow crouching.

His mind darted back to the morning. The book lady! His book picked up by mistake. His book in her basket. He rang for a nurse and almost shouted his question. "Where is the library?"

"It's not in the building, Gib," the nurse told him.

"Where is it?"

"It's a bookmobile."

"A bookmobile?"

"Yes, a library on wheels."

"When will it be back?"

"In a month."

"A month!" Gibson's voice quavered. He thought of all the things that might happen to the book, of all the things that might happen to the mare! He thought of Dr. Mills. How would he feel when he heard his book was lost?

In the month that followed, Gibson wrote a dozen letters to Dr. Mills explaining about the book, then tore each one up. He would wait until next bookmobile day. Surely the book would be returned.

Meanwhile, Time took to acting strangely again. Sometimes Gibson had to shake the clock to make sure it was running. Letters were fewer now that his father was in the heat of training. Callers were fewer now that his grandmother had a cold and his mother was caring for her.

Late one day when there had been no visitors and no letters, Tante thrust her head in the door. "You," she said, smiling with importance, "are wanted on the telephone. It's long distance!"

His bathrobe half on, his bedroom slippers flapping, Gibson followed Tante down the hall.

"Wait now until it rings," she said, waving him into the telephone booth.

He sat down on the stool, waiting, little fears and excitements stirring inside him. The bell when it came sounded like an alarm. Then the reassuring voice: "Son! I just wanted to tell you Rosalind takes her training in the spirit of play."

"Is that good, Dad?"

"Good? It's phenomenal!"

"Gee, Dad, that's great."

Now Mr. White could not keep the pride out of his voice. "Your filly's not only bridle-wise, she's whip-wise."

"How'd you do it so soon, Dad?"

"Oh," the voice chuckled, "just by tickling her with the whip along her crest. Now we can crack it and she just pricks

94

an ear as if to say, "Humph, I know where that sound comes from—no harm in that.' "

Gibson drummed his fingers up the wall at a quick trotting gait. "When she gets to racing she won't flinch at other drivers' whips, will she, Dad?"

"That's the idea of it, Son."

A brittle voice spiked into the conversation. "Your three minutes are up, sir."

"Oh, no, ma'am, we haven't talked that long. Dad—? Dad—?"

"What is it, Son?"

"You know—" A long pause. "I'd like to come home."

"I know, Son, but be game. Stick it out."

The brittle voice again, wedging in between them, pushing them apart.

"So long, Son. You'll have a letter from me tomorrow."

The letter did come and with it a whole pack of snapshots, like a moving picture. Rosalind rolling in the grass, splashing in the frog pond. Rosalind looking through a bridle, mouthing a leather bit as if it were a teething ring. Rosalind being guided with reins while Mr. White walked along behind. Rosalind sharing a meal with Bear.

Son, the letter began with a smile between the lines, *I can't quote Shakespeare like one owner I train for, but I can quote*

95

The mare's eyes looked at William Rysdyk, and he caught his own reflection in their soft reproach. 'Please, sir,' he said, turning to Mister Seely. 'Why do we got to do this?' He cast about him for some excuse and found it in the setting sun. 'Look, sir. It comes already evening. Her hock only is outgiven. She could hobble with us along to a farmhouse maybe. There I make her a bed up. Tomorrow we see how goes it with her.'

It was a long speech for William Rysdyk. He wiped the sweat from his forehead, waiting to hear what Mister Seely would say.

'Well, now,' replied Mister Seely, loosening his cravat, 'it will do no harm to wait. Hasty actions are oft regretted. Come. Let us proceed.'

The peddler whistled between his wide-set teeth. 'Crowbait!' he spat, as if the word took in men and mare both. Disgustedly, he walked over to the road, picked up his wares, and stalked off.

The first farmhouse that came into view could have been a hovel for all it mattered to the weary travelers. But it was, instead, a homey place nosing up out of lilac bushes and honeysuckle. The farmer, a tall, loose-jointed man, had to stoop a little to come out of his doorway. He walked toward them jerkily, as if his legs and arms worked from puppet strings.

After welcoming the strangers, he examined the swelling on the mare's hock. ''Pears to me like she's old and done for,' he said. 'But she's more'n welcome to a bundle of hay and a bed in my cow barn.'

'We shall be grateful to you,' Mister Seely answered tiredly.

'Tsk,' the farmer said, suddenly remembering, ''Hetty, my woman, would like fer you folks to stay, too. Our house,' he laughed, 'looks little but she bulges fer comp'ny.'

Then he thought a moment. 'You ain't asked it, I know, but we got us a pined cemetery for our own animals down the road a

98

piece.' He thumbed toward the mare. 'If she ain't better by morning, ye're welcome to my musket. And you can leave her there a-sleepin' if you got a mind to.'

'Why is it always got to be a shooting?' William Rysdyk kept asking himself as he made a warm bran poultice and tied up the mare's leg. 'Why is it?'

Neither he nor Mister Seely did justice to the plain supper of wheaten bread, fresh butter, and stewed pumpkin which the farmer's wife set out for them. And they were both up at dawn, hoping some miracle had happened in the night.

There had been no miracle. The mare lay on her side, quite still. When the men talked to her, she struggled to rise, moaning low in her throat. It was with great difficulty that William Rysdyk and the farmer boosted her to her feet.

'Rysdyk,' Mister Seely said, his face strained with emotion, 'I'm loath to ask what needs doing. But it is better this way. Better for her to sleep in a piney woods than to end her days pulling a butcher's wagon. You did not know her when she was a spirited filly, as I did. Will you do it for me? I'll saddle Sir Luddy while you are gone and meet you down the road.'

'Ach, wait! Wait!' William Rysdyk began, but this time he could think of no reason for waiting. His strength suddenly washed out of him. Never in his life had he killed an animal. He who could jack up a wagon with his hands while weaker men rolled the wheel in place, stood limp as a string of herbs.

'I'll fetch my musket,' the farmer said with a nervous jerking of his arms. He was in and out of the house, and still William Rysdyk stood.

But at last the waiting seemed worse than the doing. He made himself fasten the lead strap to the mare's halter, made himself shoulder the long-barreled musket. With set face he led her down the path between the lilacs. He watched her head bent almost to her knees, watched her hobbled, painful step. Without knowing he was doing it, he too limped to her rhythm.

When she struck the road, however, an astonishing change came over her. She began to limber up and her head lifted in interest, sifting the scents and sounds. As they went on toward the conical trees she was walking more firmly than the man who led her, almost pulling him along.

At the entrance to the little clearing in the pines, William Rysdyk halted. 'By golly!' he cried out, determination in his eyes, 'I will *not* shoot her dead. Here's a mare who will stay in the life!'

He faced about and the mare followed him back to the road, nickering when she caught sight of Sir Luddy ambling toward them. As the two horses met and snuffed nostrils, William Rysdyk looked up between Sir Luddy's ears, directly into Mister Seely's face. 'Butcher's nag goes sound, sir. She comes with us along, please could be?'

Mister Seely blew his nose loud as a trumpet, then made a soft sound in his throat as if he wanted to talk but couldn't.

'She will have it pleasant with us? Yah, sir?'

The misted eyes could only nod.

'And when deep winter comes and we have it cold and the ground lies shut and hard—she gets shelter? Yah, sir?'

'Yah it is!' Mister Seely laughed through his tears.

5: Rat-Tail Abdallah

The trip home to Sugar Loaf was slower than the trip to New York. William Rysdyk walked all the way, except downhill. Then Mister Seely dismounted and led the mare while his hired man rode Sir Luddy.

The two men had little to say to each other. There was a bond between them now that made words unnecessary. They let the mare plod along at her own pace, let her stop to rest, nodding on three legs whenever she had a mind to. Meanwhile, William Rysdyk took off his boots and yarn stockings and cooled his aching feet in the grass. After a little while man and mare would be ready to start off again.

At the journey's end it was the men and Sir Luddy who seemed travel weary. The mare appeared a little gaunt and she favored one leg, but her spirit was game.

As they turned into the Seely lane, Sir Luddy gave a loud and joyful neigh. 'Here,' he snorted quite plainly, 'is Home! Green grass growing where grass should grow and shade where shade should be and snug horse barns with doors thrown wide to the sun.'

In the weeks that followed, William Rysdyk was a boy with his first pet. He was boy and nurse and doctor too. He pulled off the mare's shoes. He trimmed her bruised and broken hoofs and rubbed them with goose grease. At night he led her down to the drainage ditch, and making a cup of his hands bathed the swollen hock with cool water. Then he turned her loose to stand barefoot in the dewy grass.

There were so many little ways in which William Rysdyk cared for the mare. He crushed her oats and ground her corn, knowing her old nippers and tushes were too worn to grind the hard kernels. And when he found she liked milk, he brought her each evening a little piggin of it, still fragrant and warm.

'Egad!' Mister Seely remarked one day as he saw her capering about in the pasture lot. 'She grows most pleasant to look upon— her coat glossed, her eye clear and bold.'

'Yah! She feeds hearty, sir,' nodded William Rysdyk proudly. 'Soon it comes time to step her on the road.'

Mister Seely ruminated a moment, roughing up his mutton-chop whiskers. 'Hook her up now, Rysdyk. We'll see how she goes.'

Once out on the road the Kent mare threw a challenge to every horse they met. She seemed unable to abide hoofbeats behind or hoofbeats ahead. She took the bit and raced down the pike as if she were trotting the Union Course. Then, with the brush over, she hobbled home, moaning in pain. It was plain to see she would never go the distances again.

And so fingers pointed and heads wagged and voices laughed to scorn. 'Ho-ho! A prize Alderney bull for a broken-down butcher's nag!' The words had a sting to them.

Winter came and the ground lay 'shut and hard' as William Rysdyk had said it would. And the mare was given shelter.

Her purple-brown eyes, sometimes vixenish, sometimes sad, laid a kind of spell on Mister Seely and his hired man. But they were alone in their feelings. The townfolk could not see in her the look of eagles. It was not given everyone to see. Even Mistress Seely regarded the Kent mare as a bad bargain, taking money from her own till, money that might better have been spent on new carpeting or tea plates, or even a fur muff.

Winter shuffled off and spring came mincing in. And one early June afternoon when William Rysdyk arrived at Sugar Loaf to do the chores, he found Mister Seely sitting on a pile of logs beside the smoke house. 'Sit down, Rysdyk,' he said, waving his arm toward the logs as if offering a fine plush chair.

William Rysdyk sat. No words were spoken. Nothing happened. Impatiently, he crossed and uncrossed his legs. He had the Jerseys and the Alderneys to bring home. The milking to do. The horse stalls to clean. Then the same chores to be done for his other employer, Mister Townsend.

'I've news,' Mister Seely said at last, taking off his hat and letting the wind pick up his milkweed hair.

'News? So?'

'Aye, my brother Ebenezer was here this day.'

What news was that! Ebenezer, a brother, comes. 'Comes he not often, sir?' William Rysdyk asked.

'Aye. But this day he had the stallion, Old Abdallah, with him.'

'Old Abdallah?'

'Old Abdallah. And this day of June, eighteen hundred and forty-eight, the Kent mare was bred to him.'

'To Old Abdallah!' William Rysdyk tried to swallow his resentment. It was done, and now no need to make questions, but in his mind he was seeing the coarse and ugly stallion, and the words spat themselves out. 'Why, he is old as the Sugar Loaf Mountain, sir.'

Mister Seely laughed hollowly. 'Not that old, Rysdyk.'

'Is he not over the twenty-five, sir?'

'Aye.'

William Rysdyk stood up. He began stripping the bark from the logs, venting his anger on them. 'The mare is a horse whereon you can be proud, sir. But Old Abdallah . . .' he could think of

103

no words strong enough. 'Old Hollow-Back! Old Rat-Tail!'

'Aye,' the answering voice was quiet.

'A big homely head he has.'

Mister Seely nodded.

'And hardly no more hairs in his tail as a naked stick.'

'I, too, have noted the scraggly tail.'

'And his temper it is fierce, sir.'

'That it is,' agreed Mister Seely, remembering.

A cat came sidling along, thinning herself against Mister Seely's legs. William Rysdyk saw Abdallah in the cat. His voice rose. 'That Abdallah has cat hams, sir.'

'So he has. I'd never thought of it just like that. But,' Mister Seely's voice firmed, 'you forget two things, Rysdyk. He can trot. And his dam was a Thoroughbred.'

The words floated over and around the hired man, unnoticed. 'And ears so big he has, with sharp points.' Suddenly William Rysdyk clapped his hands to his own ears. He smiled a little. 'I must to the chores now,' he said. 'I feel myself not good.'

Mister Seely's eyes were on the distance. 'When the colt is born, Rysdyk, you'll forget all about Old Ab. Good night.'

The hired man forced a nod. Heavy-legged, he trudged off toward the upland pasture. 'Till seeing,' he said. 'When the colt comes . . .' The words tailed off into nothing.

Fourteen

INTERRUPTIONS! Gnat-like interruptions. Little but time-suckers. Always, it seemed to Gibson, when the story was most exciting—a runaway floundering through bramble and brush, a mare going to foal—always then the book had to be laid aside. Rest. Eat. Study. But in his resting and eating and studying half of him went on with the story, building it in his mind, making it come out right.

Only when letters came from his father did the book characters slide into the past where they belonged. Then he was himself, Gibson White, owner of the filly Rosalind, bred and born to trot.

The letters all began the same, like a tune bursting because it couldn't be held in. *Your filly . . . your filly . . . your filly . . .*

Your filly's the trottingest little piece of horseflesh ever looked through a bridle.

Your filly hasn't shed the long hair under her belly, but already she knows the breaking cart is harmless as the whip.

Your filly's training to order. Took her out on the track today. She went around the turns like a hoop around a barrel!

Your filly punches her legs up and out until the rhythm kind of takes your breath. No daisy cutter, this one. Action high. It's been a long time since I've seen a youngster like her.

Your filly can count! Three times around the track and she knows it's quits—pulls toward the stable to remind me.

Your filly's game and plucky. If you as owner request we don't hurry her training, she'll be a two-minute trotter and earn her keep.

Gibson wired at once.

REQUEST YOU DO NOT HURRY ROSALIND. DON'T RUSH HER.
GIBSON WHITE

A day later his father replied.

YOUR INSTRUCTIONS RECEIVED. WE ARE PROCEEDING EASILY WITH ROSALIND. NOT DOGGING THE HEART OUT OF HER.
BEN WHITE

One afternoon when time came for Gibson to rest, he made his eyes turn away from the open hasp of the book, away from his bulletin board, too. To hurry the slow ticking of the clock, he began counting the flowers in the wallpaper. They were big cabbage roses, each with two leaves. He counted all of them, including the number of leaves. Then he began on the split flowers where the strips of paper were joined.

Suddenly he heard the knob turn quietly in the door and a voice whisper, "You awake?"

He turned to see Dr. Mills tiptoeing sheepishly into the room, as if any moment he expected a nurse to tweak him out by the ear. His glance fell on the book with the hasp open.

"Like it, Gib?"

"It's the best I ever read. Only . . . "

"Only what?"

"Only," Gibson sat up, pummeling his pillow, "I get interrupted all the time. Silly things—like papering a circular room for a Mr. Anderson who doesn't exist, and taking baths when I had one yesterday, and resting when I'm not tired."

"How far are you?"

"The Kent mare's just been bred to Old Abdallah. Does she get a good colt? Or is she too old?"

"Gib—"

"Yes, Doc?"

"Will you turn out your light a half hour earlier tonight if I let you read now?"

"Oh, Doctor Mills! Sure I will."

"Then hop to it."

6: The Foaling Spot

William Rysdyk worked in a wrath of energy, hoping the harder he worked the faster time would go; hoping, too, it would help him forget that no-account Abdallah.

Almost a year to wait for the foal!

Slowly the days piled one on top of the other. Days of stooping and lifting and dragging stones to clear a new field for Mister

Townsend. Days of plowing and cross-harrowing and pulverizing the land. Days of scattering seed until the very sockets of his arms ached. Rainy days and dusty ones. And blistering days when his beard dripped sweat. Days of making hay when he stopped only to let the work horses blow or to put the nosebag on them. He, too, was a work horse. At night when he pulled off his boots and stockings it sometimes surprised him to see feet and ankles instead of hoofs and hairy fetlocks.

The days grew shorter, cooler. Days of shocking corn. Pulling onions. Heaping turnips. Digging potatoes. Sacking them. Hauling them. Shipping them to market.

Then still and brittle days when icy branches snapped and spooked the horses. In the still days William Rysdyk chopped wood, repaired the plow irons, sharpened the harrow tines, mended harness.

So the seasons went their rounds without stint, without haste. And it was spring again. Spring with white dogwood pricking down the mountainsides and green needles of wheat piercing the soil and mallards swimming in the high creeks. Just like that it came. Spring, and the Kent mare big with foal.

One early morning of May, his dinner in a poke, William Rysdyk clicked the latch of his own gate and set out for the Seely farm. Thinking of the mare, he hastened his steps. Today he would make her stall ready. The good clean bed. The fresh straw. Today it might be. He was glad when a team and wagon pulled alongside and a family on their way to a camp meeting drove him to the Seely gate.

Even before he jumped from the wagon he felt hurried by a strange uneasiness—as if things were somehow different. Yet everything looked just as it did on any other Monday morning. Smoke feathering from the chimney. Newly hung wash skewering and bellying on the line. Chickens picking and pecking in the dooryard. Wagons standing, waiting. Everything the same. Yet somehow different.

He broke into a run, past the woodshed, the stackyard, the corncrib, past the spring house with the milk cans drying in the sun, past the chicken house, the root cellar, to the horse barn.

He looked inside. Sir Luddy was nosing above his stall door, pawing and whinnying for his breakfast. The big-faced work horses, too, were snuffling and snorting to the morning.

Of all the stalls only the mare's was open. Only she was free to come and go. Now her stall was empty. The straw untrampled. Not even a hollowed-out nest to show she had slept in it.

'Just like some other mornings,' William Rysdyk told himself. 'Yah, I know that. Often it is she sleeps in the grass.'

Yet the uneasiness hung onto him. He studied the pasture.

'Where to has she gone?' he asked. 'Not far with her bad leg,' he answered himself. 'Never does she go far.'

He picked up some sacking and ran out into the pasture. Except for a broad shadow flung across the field by three oak trees, the sun lay smooth and yellow on the grass. He tried to see into the shadow, but there was only blackness. He thought he heard the mare. He went running toward the knoll where the trees grew, calling to her as he ran. 'It comes *me!*' he cried, stumbling over the hummocky ground, leaping across the ditch. Then he slowed. He saw her now, in a spot of sun that pierced the trees.

A sigh of relief escaped him. 'She likes to neighbor with the tree trunks,' he reminded himself, 'to scratch and itch herself on the bark. But why is it the sawhorse there in the pasture? Ach, the Seely boys is up to no good, always leaving around tools and such.'

Then suddenly the four stiff legs of the sawhorse scissored.

No. It couldn't be a colt. It could be a deer? No, no.

And yet—? Could it be the little one? It's got to! Nothing else could so long-legged be. Not a dog. Not a sheep. It's got to!

'Maybe,' he said, his voice trembling, 'maybe if I sneak up by them very quiet.' He began picking his way carefully on tiptoe, then changed his mind. 'No,' he smiled into his beard, 'I'll look like I wasn't even looking.' He took a roundabout route, talking in an undertone as he walked. 'A quiet place is this for a foaling. No eyes prying. No noise. Only wind whispers.'

And now he was under the crown of shade with them. Close enough to study the new-born creature. With curious eyes the colt turned his head, his mother's milk beaded along the feelers of his muzzle like tiny seed pearls.

'Ai yai yai!' breathed William Rysdyk in awe. 'The eating is ready for him. Look on his whiskers.'

Seeing the colt, he saw more: saw in him Messenger charging down the gangplank, Silvertail trotting the highroad with a man and a boy on her back, Hambletonian with the look of eagles.

A high baby whinny interrupted his dreams. He smiled at his foolishness, fondling the creature with his eyes.

'How long you here already, little fellow?'

The nostrils fluttered in answer.

'And how pleases you our world?'

The head tossed.

'So, you high-nose our world, hmm? Or is it you have hunger?'

The mare took up with the colt, licking him a little, then snuffing noses with him, letting out a high nicker of joy.

'Hush up, mare-mom,' William Rysdyk whispered. 'Is better you quit out with that noise. Would you to have the Seely boys come out with their hollerings and jumpings and their sling-shots, maybe?'

The Kent mare liked the talk. She did not plant herself between William Rysdyk and her colt. She knew he could be trusted even when his man-hands laid hold of her young one.

'He looks bigger as any newborn, yah, mom? And he keeps his head up, no? And he looks pretty fiery.'

Gently he began rubbing the colt with the sacking. 'By golly,' he laughed as the colt struggled to free himself. 'You don't like it being rubbed? Come,' he coaxed. 'Trusting is what a colt is got to learn. Don't wiggle. What helps you that? Only a drying you get from me.'

After the rubbing, William Rysdyk clapped his hands. And to his astonishment the colt bent his knobby little knees and broke into a trot toward his mother.

'It don't hardly seem possible!' William Rysdyk sighed. 'Yesterday is a big mare only. Today is a baby trotter by her. Is more eating ready, mare-mom?'

He laughed as the colt began suckling, laughed to see the tiny tail flip-flap. 'It tastes? Hmm?' he asked.

A cow bawling to be milked broke into his happiness. He sighed again, more deeply this time. 'Who wants going to work when a colt is new borned?'

He gathered up the sacks, turning to go. 'I'll make you ready a warm mash,' he promised the mare, 'but first I must to the house to say the news.'

When William Rysdyk looked into his employer's office, Mister Seely was scowling over his ledger.

'Anything amiss?' he asked, peering over his glasses.

'Excuse, sir,' William Rysdyk began, twirling his hat nervously, 'never was anything like him.'

'Like whom? Like what, Rysdyk?'

'Like the colt, sir.'

Mister Seely laid his quill aside. 'Oh,' he said with a smile, 'so the Kent mare has foaled. Is everything all right?'

'Yah, shure, shure. Is all right. Herself she did it alone.'

'Where are they?'

'Just before the big boulder under the oak trees already.'

'A fine foaling spot. Always better foaled in the open.'

'Yah,' sighed William Rysdyk. 'With them everything is fine. The mare chawing off the grass and the colt sucking good!'

'Rysdyk!'

'Yah, sir?'

'Our Seely custom is this. Whoever spies a colt first has the naming of him.'

'How say you?' William Rysdyk gasped as if the words and their meaning were too big for understanding.

A silence came into the room. Somewhere in the house a clock bonged the hour of six. Mister Seely got up and circled the day on the wall calendar. May 5, 1849. Then he stood waiting.

William Rysdyk took a great gulp of air. 'I don't even got to think, sir! Already he's got him a name. Is Hamble-tonian!'

Mister Seely tapped his lips, thinking.

'Is too long a handle for a little feller?' William Rysdyk hurried the question.

'No, no, Rysdyk. Come to think of it, Hambletonian is just right. A name of dignity.'

Fifteen

WHAT a long handle of a name for a little foal!" Gibson chuckled, repeating the words. "Longer even than Rosalind!" He began counting the letters. H-A-M-B-L-E-T-O-N-I-A-N. Only twelve after all. Four to spare! The foal could get in the Trotting Register, too.

"Everything ties in," he said in wonderment. "Rosalind foaled on May fifth, Hambletonian's birthday, too."

He closed the book, turning the tiny gold key, thinking that with it locked it would tempt him less. Carefully he laid the little volume on the table beside his schoolbooks. How new and callow it made them look!

Even with the cover closed, Gibson was a long time coming back to himself. He had lived with the man Rysdyk for so many hours. Smiling to himself, he fingered the rolled rim of his ears to see if they had gone leprechaun. He felt of his cheeks and chin, almost expecting a wiry, sprouted beard. He dangled his legs over the side of the bed. How chalky they were! Not brawny and hairy as he imagined William Rysdyk's to be.

Before he could swing back under the covers, the door opened and a nurse entered. "That's right," she said. "Dangle 'em a while. Then walk around, up and down the halls. To-morrow we're moving you into a cottage in a room with three other boys. You're getting so much better," she went on as she whisked off the pillow slips. "Besides, we must have this quiet room for someone who really needs it."

It took two men to move all Gibson's belongings. They had to make a special trip for the bulletin board, covering it with a bedsheet to protect the pictures. They hung it in the cottage to the right of Gibson's bed. This gave his roommates a better over-all view, but at least he was closest to it.

Gibson felt shy as he stood inside the new room while a nurse introduced him. "Gib White," she said, "I want you to meet Beaver Teeth. He occupies the bed on your left." Then in the midst of her introductions she was called away.

"His name's really McCarthy," explained the boy across from Gibson, "but we dubbed him Beaver Teeth for two very good reasons."

Beaver Teeth grinned obligingly, showing the reasons. "Let me introduce to you," he said with a sweep of his hand toward the bed opposite, "Grubber Thompson. Last summer he worked in his dad's grocery store in Norfolk. Grubbed up the boats that stopped there. Now he makes miniature trains for all the kids he knows, and for some he don't."

Grubber, freckled and copper-haired, put down a pair of long-nosed pliers. "Hi, Gib," he smiled.

115

"To his left," Beaver went on with his tour, "and directly opposite your bed, meet Pat Jones. He's our paint dauber. We call him Mike, short for Michelangelo."

"Say, Gib," asked Mike, looking at the bulletin board, "what do they call those racing rigs?"

And with that question Gibson felt at home. "Sulkies is what they're called," he replied.

"Sulkies? Why on earth call 'em that?"

"It's a legend," Gibson explained. "Pop Geers told Dad that once there was a driver who wanted to be alone; so he made himself a one-man cart. His wife told him only a sulky man'd ride alone. The name stuck."

Later, sitting up in bed with his history book on his knees, Gibson found himself listening instead of studying. He had been alone so long he couldn't concentrate. Yet Beaver, studying to be an architect, seemed able to write and design and still join in the banter that bounced from bed to bed.

For a week Gibson did not unlock his book. It was a world so far away and yet so close he could only feel but never speak

116

of it. What if the boys were to make fun of the padlock and key? Or of the long-bodied horse on the cover?

How was he ever to finish the book? Sometimes he thought about writing Dr. Mills, asking for a single room again. And then he realized he would miss this new companionship. The questions about Rosalind. The games of checkers after supper. He would even miss the pleasant clutter of freight cars hooked together on the window sills, and Mike's paintings drying all over the place, and Beaver's blueprints and his talk about the kind of hospital he would design some day.

Then one morning everything solved itself. The book-mobile lady came in with two mystery stories apiece for Beaver and Mike. With the stories on hand, quiet settled down over the cottage in the trees. The only sounds were made by the distant chatter of squirrels and by Grubber snipping a piece of wire with his shears.

Nobody was paying any attention to Gibson. Quickly his fingers were feeling in the saddlebag, finding the book, unlocking the gold hasp. With a sigh of satisfaction he settled into the pillows.

7: Son of Old Abdallah

William Rysdyk heard the clatter of hoofs above the noise of his sledge hammer. He looked down from the upland pasture where he was repairing fence.

A carriage drawn by two high-stepping blacks came whipping around the bend at full speed with a spotted coach dog running

in attendance. As the horses turned into the Seely lane, William Rysdyk raced downhill, arriving just in time to catch the reins.

Suddenly the dooryard came alive. Geese clacking at the coach dog. The coach dog barking at the Seely cats. The blacks neighing and bugling to the Kent mare, whose outline they saw in the distance.

William Rysdyk studied the men as they climbed from the carriage. Two he recognized. Big John Doughty, the banker, and Israel Toothill, owner of the ironworks. Two he had never seen. One was a little snipe of a man with a slender bill nose pointing downward. The other was pranked out in a tight-waisted carriage coat with elegant buttons, big as twenty-dollar gold pieces. The coat was too warm for the day. The man within steamed like the horses, his waved forelock clinging damply to his face.

'Gentlemen,' Mister Seely shouted above the din, 'I am deeply honored. You find me in my house slippers, about to join Mistress Seely in the evening meal. You will sup with us, of course?'

The man with the long bill of a nose squinted up at the sun. 'Afraid not, Seely,' he said, his voice full of high harsh notes. 'We've one more stop to make before sundown.'

William Rysdyk took a long time tying the lines to the hitching post. Ain't only one man, he thought, it's four. It wonders me. Maybe only they are going to build up a new schoolhouse. But maybe . . . it could be the colt!

He felt a jerking at his farm frock. Turning, he saw the youngest Seely boy, his mouth full of green apple but talking anyway, spouting a volley of questions.

'Sh!' William Rysdyk raised his forefinger, pressing it against his pursed lips. He ran into the tool shed and came out with the grindstone and scythe, setting the stone as near the huddle of men as he dared.

'Yourself you turn it,' he whispered to the boy. 'Watch how the sparks spritz when I make sharp the blade.'

The boy turned the crank, fascinated by the flinty sparks. The noise was only a little noise. William Rysdyk could listen now.

'We are a committee of four,' the banker was saying as he centered the diamond pin in his neckcloth, 'and it is our pleasurable duty to line up entries for the matinee trotting races in New York City this fall.'

Mister Seely's thumbs were in his trouser pockets, his eyes on Sugar Loaf Mountain, blue-humped in the distance. 'Gentlemen, I'm afraid we have no entries this year. Sir Luddy is just a middling goer.' He looked from one face to another. 'Not since the days of Silvertail have we had a horse that could go the pace and stay the distance. But while you gentlemen are here, I'd be honored with your opinion on a colt by Old Abdallah out of the granddaughter of Silvertail. He's rising four months now.'

'Hmmm . . .' the driver in the splendid coat unbuttoned his

119

enormous gold buttons. He took his watch from his waistcoat and opened it. He showed it to Mister Doughty, the banker.

Four watches came out, the minutes compared.

The decision seemed to rest with Mister Toothill, the iron-monger, as all eyes fastened on him. William Rysdyk studied the man. He was built much like a kangaroo, stout of trunk and leg, with a head that pinched up into nothing as if all the strength had gone into the body. 'We could spare ten minutes,' he said.

'Come along, Rysdyk!' Mister Seely called, 'and bring a measure of oats with you. Son, you may come, too.'

The men waited, talking about the rain needed, about the Erie Railroad to New York. 'Why, she averages nigh twenty miles an hour!' one was saying when William Rysdyk came up to them.

'Rysdyk is my right hand,' Mister Seely explained. 'He's the only one who can catch the colt.'

The men looked at the patched homespun trousers, at the pointed ears, as they followed along, trying without success to keep up with the long strides of Mister Seely's hired man.

Under the oak trees the mare and the colt stood head to tail, switching flies for each other. But when they saw a drove of strangers coming at them, they trotted off like sparks of fire.

William Rysdyk walked away from the fleeing pair, looking skyward as if seeking birds instead of horses to grain. Gradually the colt and the mare changed their course, coming now at a walk toward him. 'I will lay out the way it is,' he told them. 'Now comes a bunch of men. They just stand and look and only make talk. Then they give each other the hand. I don't care for it too, but soon is over. Yah?'

The words were so low pitched the mare and the colt had to come near and nearer to catch the ups and downs in his voice. Step by step they came until he could lay hold on the colt's halter. He offered each a palmful of oats for obedience. Then he led the colt to the men, the mare following.

'Father!' the Seely boy screamed. 'I'm going to be sick!'

Mister Seely excused himself and walked very swiftly toward the outhouse, towing the boy. 'Too many green apples,' he muttered under his breath.

With Mister Seely gone, the men turned their attention on the colt. They spoke freely, as if the hired man were deaf and dumb. But their remarks hit him across the face, lightly at first, then in sharp whiplashes.

'Too high on the legs,' said the banker, pulling his plaid waistcoat over his paunch. 'No elegance of form.'

'Rough made, I should say,' piped Henry Spingler, the little snipe of a man. 'Note how ungraceful the neck, how large and coarse the head.'

'And the ears!' agreed the greatcoated gentleman, stifling a laugh, 'long and pointed, like those of a donkey.'

'His hips appear higher to me than his shoulders,' Mister Toothill put in. 'And his tail a mere switch.'

Their words lashed on, cutting deeper and deeper.

'Might make a chunk horse for hauling heavy loads,' Mr. Doughty offered.

Fat puffy hands and big-knuckled skinny ones felt all the way down the colt's legs, felt of his hindquarters.

'Cat hams!' pronounced the banker.

William Rysdyk caught his breath. His very own words snapping back at him!

Now the men were laughing and joking, clapping each other on the back. 'He couldn't beat a calf in a mile and a half,' said one.

' "If the leaven's no good," ' Henry Spingler recited, ' "the loaf won't rise, and if the sire's coarse, the colt's likewise." '

The man with the handsome coat elbowed the ironmonger. 'Apt to be a stumblebum,' he roared in laughter. 'Apt to trip over every molehill.'

William Rysdyk let his gaze travel over the colt. To him he was all power and pride. Hips higher than shoulders? Yah, shure. To give speed. Switch tail? Yah, shure. Still a suckling he is. Give the little feller time. In every bone and fiber he saw strength and power. No weakness anywhere. He looked at the tiny star on the forehead, no bigger than a snowflake. He glanced now at the overdressed men, their diamond scarf pins, their gold buttons.

'Ach!' He clenched his fist. 'In their looking glasses they should be looking! Needle legs and scrapbag bodies and darning-egg heads!'

The colt, too, seemed annoyed by the talk. He leaned toward the men, his mouth opening now in a great cavernous yawn. In that simple gesture he dismissed them and their fribbling.

When Mister Seely rejoined the group, the men sheared their words like women trimming off the extra crust from a pie.

'He's the son of Old Abdallah, all right,' the banker said.

'Yes, sir!' the others agreed. 'The son of Old Abdallah. No mistaking.'

On the way back to the house the greatcoated man had a trifling accident. He caught his instep-strap on a tree root, and when it snagged free that august gentleman went flat on his buttons in the drainage ditch. He made quite a splash.

It was fortunate for William Rysdyk that a blasting toot from the evening train coincided with the loud explosion of his laughter. 'Who now is the stumblebum?' he muttered to himself.

Later, in the stackyard with the men gone, he was still chuckling over the incident. But as he stood atop the strawstack pitching down the straw, an idea fastened itself on his mind. Slowly, thoughtfully, he thrust the pitchfork into the stack, the tines going in deep.

'Maybe,' his eyes narrowed in thought, 'there is maybe a scheme in the men. It's maybe they think I tell Mister Seely so they buy the colt cheap.'

The more he thought about it, the more the idea festered. The committee must have liked Hambletonian. 'High on the legs means leggy,' he kept saying as he finished his chores. 'Leggy colt means speed. Yah! It now comes sharp to me. They make a donkey of Hambletonian for to buy him cheap.'

After this visit whenever a stranger came to the Seely place, William Rysdyk was in a panic. He hid the colt and the mare in the spattered shade of the oak trees, tying them there so they couldn't trot out and show bright bay against the green. Then he managed to work within earshot of the visitor. But his work was wasted. If he culled potatoes, he put the little ones with the big. If he split wood for the kitchen, it turned out to be kindling instead of stove wood. If he cleaned stalls, he threw out the clean straw instead of the soiled.

Men did come to look at the colt. Some poked fun at the big ears and the Abdallah head. Others just looked and said little. It was these who worried William Rysdyk most. One night when he had finished his chores, he could stand it no longer.

'I can't hold it out!' he told the colt. 'Some way I got to buy you.'

Sixteen

WITHOUT turning his head, Gibson's eyes darted around
the room. Mike and Beaver were still deep in their books.
Grubber was studying a half-finished gondola on his work
table.

Gibson glanced at his clock. Almost eleven. Soon the door
would swing open and four lunch trays would come in, one
atop another. If he read fast—another chapter, perhaps. Sound-
lessly he turned the page, and just that quickly crossed from
one world to the other.

8: Colt=at=Heel

Before his courage petered away, William Rysdyk marched swiftly to the kitchen door of the Seely residence. His mind was made up! He washed his face and hands at the pump, dousing the cold water over his head, taking a great mouthful of it, then fountaining it over a dusty bed of catmint. With awkward fingers he smoothed his hair and combed his beard. He cleaned his boots on the scraper. Then, shivering in excitement, he presented himself at the door.

'The gentleman is in?' he asked the hired girl.

Mehitabel Tiffet had a voice with a growl in it. 'He ain't done with his coffee,' she said, eyeing him sharply.

'I wait here by the well. I got to speak private with him.'

As he waited, playing his finger along the coiled rope, he tried to plan what he would say. Why is it? he thought. With the animals in the fields, I feel myself big. To lift, no stones is too heavy. To dig, no ditches is too deep. But, ach, inside houses I shrink myself. Even my muscles weazen down little. To pea size they get.

He squirmed, toeing his foot against the well, feeling small and green and young.

The door opened and a hand flung out, holding a plate. 'Leftovers!' the voice of Mehitabel barked, 'but they help stay the hunger.'

William Rysdyk took the food. A gray slice of mutton had gone cold and tallowed to the plate. Beside it humped a cold potato. He tried to eat, but the tallow reminded him of the goose grease he used on the horses' hoofs.

Looking around and seeing no one in the gathering dusk, he put the plate at his feet. Then low in his throat, so Mehitabel would not hear, he called, 'Come, kitling, kitling, kitling.'

A barn cat streaked out from the shadows, followed by a parade of four little kittens with stove-poker tails. They maneuvered for position around the plate, then sharp white teeth went to work and four little penwiper tongues and one big one swabbed the plate clean.

As Mehitabel's footsteps came thudding to the door, William Rysdyk snatched up the plate, scattering the cats back into the shadows.

'Kinder hungry, wasn't ye?' Mehitabel's voice softened as she took the plate. 'The mister—he is done with his coffee now. Has to have his three cups every night. Come in.'

William Rysdyk walked quickly through the kitchen, his nostrils wrinkling at the smells of vinegar and mutton. He followed the direction flag of Mehitabel's finger through a dark hallway to a brightly glowing room. He took one step across the threshold, then stood frozen in the doorway, like a rabbit cornered by a beam of light.

A lamp burning with an uneven flame made a white pool on the desk, then flung great shadows on the wall. One of the shadows was Mister Seely winding the wag-on-the-wall clock, pulling down the weight cord.

As William Rysdyk waited, hesitating, the youngest Seely

boy brushed past him and burst into the room. 'Father! Look at the pictures I made.'

Mister Seely turned around, surprise in his look. 'Oh,' he said, spying William Rysdyk over the head of his son, 'come to the light and see the pictures.'

'What for pictures have you?' the hired man asked the boy, with no question in his voice at all. How could he hold his mind on pictures? His eyes looked through them, seeing the colt instead, the big promise in him. A stallion grown. Muscles bulging. Veins big and branching like rivers on a map.

Mister Seely duteously praised the pictures and dismissed the boy. 'Now then.' His eyes went to William Rysdyk's as he settled himself comfortably in a chair by the desk. He picked up his pen, fluting the feather with his thumb, and waited, smiling.

'In your office-room, sir,' William Rysdyk stammered, 'I wouldn't want to bother you.'

'No bother, Rysdyk. Speak up.'

But suddenly the man could not speak, nor even breathe. There was a tightness in his chest and the room seemed to be closing in on him. If he were only out of doors! 'Can you, sir—can you once to the pasture lot come?'

'Is anything wrong?'

'No, no. Is everything fine.'

'Then whatever it is, Rysdyk, say it here.'

Say it here, say it here, the clock repeated. And then suddenly the tight feeling in his chest gave way and the words came tumbling out like water over a mill wheel.

'The colt, sir!' he cried. 'The colt! Before comes another man to look, I should buy him!'

'You? You? Buy him?'

'Yah, sir. *Who else?*' William Rysdyk nodded vehemently.

'The committee, they make little of him. His ears. Donkey ears. I got donkey ears, too.'

He came close to Mister Seely, placing one hand on the desk. 'I was godoopt, ach, I mean baptized, here in America. I was godoopt for William of Orange, the same one where Orange County got its name. But I am a Dutchman. Of me everybody makes little. Of the colt, too.' He took a deep breath, then blurted, 'Is it fine with you if I buy?'

Mister Seely's gaze went to the ceiling. He found a box-elder bug in the splash of light and sat staring at the bug as if it got in the way of his thinking.

'I make a question, sir,' reminded William Rysdyk. 'Couldn't I got an answer?'

The box-elder bug fell to the desk, Mister Seely's eyes falling with it. 'Where would you stable him?' he asked.

'My chicken shed, sir, what Mister Townsend give me, I going to fix up into a barn.'

'And what are your plans for the colt?'

'I drive him. And the wind, she whistles by our donkey ears. And we whistle by . . .' William Rysdyk's blue eyes danced with a sudden idea. 'And we whistle by Mister Toothill and Mister Doughty and the man what looks like a snipe bird.' He laughed deep in his throat.

'What if the colt prove slow and sluggish?'

'It couldn't be.'

'You expect both speed and stamina?'

'How could it else? He is deep made in his heart place.'

'Pull up a chair and sit down, Rysdyk. Let us ponder a moment.'

The chair scraped across the carpet. William Rysdyk perched himself on the edge of it. 'My mind is up-made,' he said hoarsely. 'The littler feller gets into me here, sir.' He patted his linsey-

woolsey shirt. 'If he goes from the pasture lot . . .' His eyes studied a crimson rose in the carpet.

'What then?'

'Then'—the hired man's voice trembled and his beard quivered—'I would like the meadowlark be. The meadowlark who comes back to her field and finds her nest and younkers plowed under by rough hands. Only,' he sighed after a little silence, 'the meadowlark could sing herself out of the pain. With me it only could stay inside here.'

'Come, come, Rysdyk. I must admit I've been thinking of selling, but you are carrying your dreams too far.'

There! He knew it! The boss was going to sell. William Rysdyk hurried his words. 'I got a little money, sir, but you give no answer. Could I buy or couldn't I buy?'

Mister Seely let his mind go back to the gold pieces he had paid out for the crippled mare. He turned down the wick of the lamp as if his thoughts might show in his face. She might have a better colt in the future, he was thinking. Maybe one. Maybe two. The postmaster had already offered seventy-five dollars for her. As for the son of Old Abdallah, he might bring a hundred dollars, odd-looking as he was.

He watched the box-elder bug swing up on his paper cutter. His thoughts went on to the drought, to the crops drying. There would be none of the little extras from New York this year. Only the necessaries.

Aloud he said, 'The winter will be lean.'

'By my place I am already tucked in good, sir. Roots and apples in the cellar already. What matters it to eat beans of last year's growth?'

Mister Seely did not answer for a long time. 'I would have to sell the mare, too,' he said at last. 'Ever since she came limping through the gate, Mistress Seely has been twitting me to sell her. Yes, they would both have to go. The mare with colt-at-heel.'

William Rysdyk leaped to his feet. 'By golly! Is better still! Mare-mom too!' He mouthed the sound of the words, 'Colt-at-heel, colt-at-heel.' He began reaching into his pockets, but all he had in them, he knew, were three big copper pennies and a handkerchief, quite dirty.

'I have alone but three coppers with me,' he said, 'but by my chicken shed in an old teapot I got twenty-five taler.'

A smile of pity played about Mister Seely's lips. 'I could let you have one of the work horses for that,' he said, 'but for the mare and colt it would be one hundred and fifty dollars.'

The house noises suddenly grew loud and distinct. A rocker creaking on a loose floorboard. Mice skittering in the walls. Against these little noises the hard metal dollars jangled in William Rysdyk's head.

'A hundred and fifty taler!'

'For twenty-five dollars you could have the work horse, Rysdyk. He has perhaps fifteen good years left in him. Perhaps twenty.'

The words were lost. A hundred and fifty taler! The hired man sighed deeply, then rose from his chair.

'Rysdyk!' Irritation showed in Mister Seely's voice, but it was as if he were irritated with himself, too. 'Rysdyk,' he repeated, 'you would be better off with the work horse. And I would be better off selling the pair to a pleasantly situated farmer. He could get one or two foals from the mare, and the colt would make him a good wagon horse.'

Over and over William Rysdyk turned the coppers in his hand. 'They look so few,' he said, discouragement heavy in his voice. 'Couldn't you a little cheaper make it?'

The annoyance in Mister Seely's voice grew. 'One hundred and twenty-five is my limit. If I sell at that figure, I am beetle-headed. If you buy at that figure, you are. The work horse, now . . .'

'Better I go home, sir, and put the head on the pillow. After a sleep I know for sure.'

In the morning William Rysdyk did know. It was sunup and the two men stood facing each other in the barnyard. Morning lay wet on the fence rails and on the leaves of the trees.

'My mind, it is up-made, sir!' William Rysdyk said with a resolute look in his eye. 'Only one question I could want to ask.'

Mister Seely waited.

'The money it grows slow. With the wages of ten dollars a month from you and six dollars from Mister Townsend, how long time I got to pay?'

'As long as you like, Rysdyk,' Mister Seely said kindly. It hurt him to take the money at all. But he had set his price. 'I'm glad the two will be with you,' he added.

As William Rysdyk counted out twenty-five silver dollars, a faraway look came into Mister Seely's eyes. 'Where the ramp meets the barn door,' he said, 'a secret vault lies beneath. There, wrapped in a worn hearth rug and covered with a piece of oiled cloth, is Silvertail's saddle. It now belongs to you.'

Slowly Mister Seely turned and walked into the house and up the stairs. He stood by the upper hall window and watched his hired man disappear into the vault. He watched him come out with Silvertail's saddle and lay it on the mare's back. Watched him ride out of the lane with a colt skittering along at heel.

For a long time he stood there until the three creatures smalled and were lost to view.

Seventeen

GIBSON sighed as though William Rysdyk's worry and relief had been his. Then a change came over his face, a look of doubt and questioning. Quickly he leafed back through the book to the title page. The words he sought were there. His finger underscored them—"a true account of the origin, history, and characteristics of Rysdyk's Hambletonian." It was true! The author wasn't telling a tall tale just to amuse himself. William Rysdyk, the Kent mare, Hambletonian, were real.

The door opened now, and a nurse wheeled in a cart with four trays, one atop the other. Gibson's laughter rocked through the cottage as he saw what was on them—boiled potatoes and slices of mutton, for all the world like the plate of Mehitabel Tiffet. Only this food was hot. Little feathers of steam curled up from each plate. Now he could tell the boys about his book. It was true!

After they ate, he read snatches of the story to them, and it seemed even better for the sharing.

The days now fell away in a beehive of busyness. There was a kind of comfort in doing things together. Mike swishing and daubing and making pictures for anyone who so much as glanced at his work. Beaver buried in blueprints. Grubber soldering and snipping and talking big of signal towers and switch points. Gibson at his bulletin board, rearranging the pictures to get more on, poring over the entries in his ledger, working problems, sending his school papers back to Lexington. And all the boys coming to his mother and grandmother

with buttons to be sewed on and worries to be cleared up.

Having roommates was better than rooming alone. Tricks and pranks seemed to make the food taste better, and riddles going from bed to bed in the dark made sleep come sooner. Letters and birthday boxes and even visitors were shared.

But in all Gibson did, half of him was left behind on the road to Chestertown, riding a bay mare with colt-at-heel. Even in the news about Rosalind his kinship with William Rysdyk strengthened. Rysdyk would have understood what Gibson's father meant when he wrote:

Your filly's ticking off eighths, quarters, and halves at a 2:30 clip. We're avoiding top speed, however, remembering owner's instructions not to hurry her.

Your filly doesn't like mud flying on her. She prefers to set the pace. But we're teaching her to be a come-from-behind horse, too.

Your filly's wind is improving. Her pipes are open.

Your filly's coming fast. She went a short sweet brush today.

Your filly's learning to score down and take off with a field of veterans.

Your filly's learning to trot near the rail and away from the rail and in the middle of the pack. So wherever she finds herself in a race she should feel at home.

Your filly seems to know trotting is the business of her life.

Your filly steps off gaily and takes her work with a relish.

Your filly responds. Turn her head the right way of the track and she'll fly. Turn her in the opposite direction and she just saunters along.

Often the book lay untouched for days, waiting for an hour when Mike and Grubber and Beaver would be absorbed in their own lives. The next time came just after his mother and grandmother had returned home. It was a day of rain, a hard-driven rain rip-rapping on the roof, plashing at the window panes, tittle-tattling on the tin of the eavestrough, rushing down the spout, then deadening itself in the earth.

Voices were lost in the din of it, and minds went burrowing into their own tunnels like moles.

Gibson dug into his saddlebag. His hand found the book, and his nose smelled of it. The dampness had brought out the nice leathery aroma. With eager fingers he opened to his place.

9: Rysdyk's Big Bull

The Kent mare with colt-at-heel faced the morning and the bigness of it. It belonged to them. The whole of it. Earth and sky and mountain, and leaves swirling and goldfinches swinging on weed stems until a body dizzied just watching. Sometimes a madcap wind tossed a shower of hickory nuts on their heads. This sent the colt scampering off until his mother whickered him back.

There was so much for the colt to do! Milkweed fluff to blow to smithers, blinking frogs to out-stare, then to flip with his muzzle until he jumped them out of sight.

'Ai yai yai,' sighed William Rysdyk as he slid down from the mare's back to lead her a while. 'Hambletonian and mare-mom. *It ain't only one kind of joy, it's two!*'

They passed houses with featherbeds airing and houses sending out spicy odors of fall preserving, passed cornfields with men shocking corn and gangs of blackbirds squawking over dropped kernels. But William Rysdyk neither saw nor heard nor smelled autumn. For his eyes there was only the colt trotting beside his mother, for his ears only the patter of hoofs on the road, for his nostrils only the good warm smell of the sun on their bodies.

At home with his colt and mare, William Rysdyk fell to work with dogged energy. 'That Dutchman is touched in the head,' his neighbors said as they gaped over their fences, watching him toil and sweat for the lame mare and the overbig colt. They watched him make a foundation of stones on the slope of a hill, wondering why he piled the stones so high in front and so low against the hill. When he moved the sloping-roofed chicken shed and set it on the foundation, then they knew.

'It got to be high roofed for mare-mom now and for Hamble-tonian when he gets big,' William Rysdyk told the curious. 'And if it got chicken lice, I end them,' he said, pouring boiling water over lye ashes and brooming the walls with fierce pleasure.

As a crowning touch he thatched the roof for warmth in winter and coolness in summer. When the work was done he stood proud, as a brood-mare face and a young quizzical one looked out upon their master. 'Is snug!' he said. 'Rough-made but not leaky. By criminy! A colt here can be happy like anything!'

'Hmpf!' the neighbors snorted. 'He looks more bull than colt.' And behind the Dutchman's back and to his face, the colt became known as 'Rysdyk's Big Bull.'

The more they taunted, however, the more firmly the man believed in the greatness of his colt, and the harder he trained him. Up before the stars faded, teaching him to whoa, leading him at the trot. Faster and faster each morning, until both man and colt grew hard-muscled and deep-lunged.

As for the mare, she seemed to grow younger with the months. When anyone came near, both she and her colt would strike a trot for the pure love and excitement of speed.

Always late at night after chores, William Rysdyk hied himself to the little hillside barn with old salt sacks for rub rags. There he would curry and groom until two coats shone glossy bright. Sometimes when he had finished rubbing Hambletonian's coat he stood back in awe, reluctant to run his rough fingertips across it for fear of snagging the satin.

With two creatures dependent on him, William Rysdyk's work had a new strength and purpose. Sleeves rolled, he faced each season like a giant refreshed—splitting logs, hauling, plowing as if he were made of iron. Isaac Townsend's and Jonas Seely's acres began yielding more wheat, more rye, more corn. This pleased them so greatly they gave their hired hand a Jersey milch cow and a red Holstein.

And each month the money-till in the teapot was opened and silver dollars tucked inside. Soon the debt would be paid. Soon the mare and colt would be William Rysdyk's. Only once did he dip into his savings. A beautiful white martingale hanging from the ceiling in the general store seemed made for the colt.

'Maybe this I buy for the Fair, not knowing, yet knowing,' he chuckled as he fastened it on Hambletonian.

It was a September day, and without any more thought, without any planning, he entered Hambletonian, now two years old, in the Orange County Fair. **The** whole idea came on him suddenly. He knew he owned the best two-year-old in the county; it was high time others knew.

When it came William Rysdyk's turn to show his colt, the judges shouted, 'Make way! Make way!' And indeed the warning was needed. Men, women, children jumped back in alarm to escape the flying heels. Lead rein in hand, William Rysdyk ran up and down showing his colt at the trot. He forgot he was at the Fair. He forgot everything in the rhythm of his colt's trot. Side by side they went, man and horse, evenly matched, not wanting to whoa. Not either of them.

It was the judge, cupping his hands to his mouth, bellowing like a bull, that called a halt. 'Whoa!' he roared. *'First prize in the two-year-old stallion class to Hambletonian by Abdallah.'*

The crowd stood stunned as the blue ribbon and the five-dollar premium went to William Rysdyk. Their mouths were opened, their hands rigid at their sides. They could not applaud. When at

last their tongues loosed, they said, 'Oh—him,' pointing to the colt. 'The judge has been taken in by the white martingale and the *man's* endurance. Does the ribbon stand for speed? No! Does it stand for style? Sakes, no! Not with only two other stallions in the competition.' They laughed in relief.

And so the blue ribbon added little to the colt's fame. Not even in the eyes of his owner. William Rysdyk already knew his horse was best.

With the five-dollar premium he bought an old, dilapidated gig with a hub and two spokes missing. After seeing to its repair and building a box on it, he used it to deliver milk to the Erie Railroad for Mister Seely, Mister Townsend, and himself. The colt, frisky and green, trotted between the shafts.

'I get a color when I think it is you I drive to a milk wagon,' William Rysdyk confided in him on their first trip. 'But look once,' he said to the pricked ears, 'how it with us stands. Soon the old tea-pot gets heavy with silver. Soon is all fixed up with Mister Seely, and you I own. Outright! Then will you have it pleasant with me.'

The third time out, Hambletonian looked as comfortable in harness as he did in halter. He was jogging down the main pike, full of play as a kitten, shaking his head and bugling to the morning. Behind him, in the box of the cart, the milk cans made a pleasant rattling.

Suddenly, halfway between Sugar Loaf and Chestertown, he felt a few drops of rain on his nose. They were big drops. Big and far apart at first. Then a wind came up and the rain smalled and needled, pricking him, now on the back, now on the face.

He asked William Rysdyk to go. As plainly as it is given a horse to talk, he said, 'Let's step! To the station to dump the milk cans. Then home! Home to the snug hillside barn, with hay wisping out of the rack.'

'Yah, shure!' William Rysdyk answered the colt, for the rain dripped from his hat brim and now was running coldly down his neck. And the wind kept lifting his wet beard, slapping it across his face. 'Yah, shure!' he agreed. 'Is better we should go!'

And go they did. Like eels through water. The countryside swam past them. The pike was theirs. Beckoning to them, curling a finger at them. Then in a flash of lightning they saw a blur in the distance. A humpbacked blur crawling on the road, crawling like some beetle. Only bigger. Blacker. Blocking the pike.

'Over-catch it!' cried William Rysdyk, and Hambletonian bore down on the beetly thing. It was a gig! Shiny new, drawn by a high-stepping black. Rain sheeted over the blackness of it, over the black umbrella of the driver, over the black back of the horse.

Hambletonian wanted to be rid of it, to get around it, to kick rain in its face.

But the black thing was black in spirit, too. It hogged the center of the pike, lurching with laughter at the ditches on either side, the ditches deep and slippery with rain.

Now Hambletonian was breathing on the beetle's back, prodding it with his breath. Unless it flew away, he was going to trot right over it, smashing its shiny shell. William Rysdyk's mouth went open to cry 'Whoa!' But the word died on his lips. For to his left a farmer's lane came out, broadening to meet the road. Perhaps they could pass the black beetle there. Perhaps.

Now the colt saw it, too, now felt his right rein slacken, felt a tightening of his left, felt his head turning the way he wanted to go! The way was his! With twenty-foot strides he caught the black just as he hit the widened place in the road, then whipped around him, back onto the pike, the cart teetering wildly. 'Hurrah!' cried William Rysdyk. 'You done it!' And the milk cans rattled and applauded in the box.

141

In the midst of a hurrah William Rysdyk glanced back.
The man jouncing under the umbrella was long-nosed Henry
Spingler! At the self-same instant Mister Spingler caught as in a
glare of light the dilapidated gig, the teetering milk cans, the
beard strangely familiar, and the big-eared colt. His back stiffened.
A chunk horse passing his black! A chunk horse a pacemaker
for him!

He slapped the lines, lifted them, lifting the black's head,
yelling to him, yelling at him, roaring with the thunder.

'So big a noise from so little a man!' laughed William Rysdyk.

And now the black began to step, lengthening his stride, settling to business.

Hambletonian pounded on, his ears laced back, tormented by
the oncoming hoofbeats. Down the main street of Chestertown,
past the inn, past the church, the bank, the postoffice, the general
store they raced, the black still trailing. Bankers, printers, store-
keepers came running out, bareheaded in the rain. The din was
ear-splitting. Hoofs clattering. Milk cans clinking. Voices cheer-

ing, some for Rysdyk's Big Bull, and some for the black.

'By golly,' exclaimed William Rysdyk, 'the speed comes sooner as I think! A colt making challenge to Mister Spingler's horse!' A wild ecstasy poured through him as he felt the give and take between Hambletonian's mouth and his own hand. 'Maybe his hips *is* higher as his shoulders? Maybe so. What else gives the pushing power? *What else?*'

For a full mile Main Street ran straight as a whiffletree, then turned sharply to the right along the Erie tracks to the station. The road was wide enough for a good brush, wide enough for horses to go abreast, for horses to pass. But there was no passing. Hambletonian was mighty as the storm. He was a bolt of lightning, fearing nothing, driven by the thunder of his own speed. The black lumbered along behind, as if Mister Spingler were an anchor around his neck.

They were nearing the turn now and William Rysdyk took a quick glance over his shoulder. He saw Mister Spingler reach for the whip, saw him crack it across his horse's rump, saw at the same instant the wind whoosh under the umbrella and blow it inside out.

Hambletonian saw it, too. He made a shying jump, then caught his trot. But the black, frightened out of his wits, broke into a wild gallop, broke free of the shafts, and streaked for home. The gig, however, slurred on, making a beeline for a bed of canna lilies at the door of the station. It wound up there, very still, with one wheel off. And poking up very pertly between its spokes were canna lilies, red and yellow.

As William Rysdyk reined in, he looked back amazed. Mister Spingler, in top hat, was sitting in the flower bed, sitting quite upright in what was left of the gig. And in his hand he held, like a torch, the inside-out umbrella.

143

Eighteen

GIBSON burst into hilarious laughter. He glanced up to see the rain still washing against the panes. And if he peered into the grayness of it, he could see quite plainly the ramrod figure of Mister Spingler sitting among the lilies.

"Hey, Gib!" Beaver called above the rain. "Why don't you get through with *One Man's Horse* and let me ride him a while?"

With thumb and fingers Gibson felt the fewness of the pages left to him. "Only a little more to go," he said wistfully. Then he began laughing again. "I think William Rysdyk's in for a peck of trouble."

"What kind of trouble?"

"I don't know, but he just made a monkey of Henry Spingler's big black."

"Who's Henry Spingler?"

"He's the town bigwig."

"Well, find out what happens so I can have the book."

Beaver's words were wasted. Gibson had already turned the page.

10: Mister Spingler Hurls a Challenge

Mister Spingler was not one to forget. At dusk that very evening he appeared in the doorway of William Rysdyk's cowshed. Behind him was the committee—John Doughty, Israel Toothill with dog at heel, and Mister Dandy, the driver, wearing a coat much less elegant.

'Ahem,' coughed Mister Spingler.

William Rysdyk was milking his red Holstein at the time, and the sound startled him so completely he almost upset his milkpail. He stumbled to his feet, remembering his manners.

'How make you it?' he asked the men politely.

Mister Spingler ignored the question. He inserted two fingers between the buttons of his waistcoat. 'You may finish your milking,' he said. 'Then we would have a word with you.'

Two more squirts and the pail was full. William Rysdyk now poured the steaming milk into a can, lowered it into a tank of water, and came over to the waiting men.

'We have come,' Mister Spingler announced, 'to see the colt. Be so good as to trot him out.'

Slowly William Rysdyk walked across the pasture lot to the barn, wondering what the men could want. Still more slowly he opened the door of the colt's stall, standing proudly to one side as the horse charged out like Messenger down the gangplank.

With nostrils distended he sampled the air. Then he trotted across the grassy plot as if his legs had springs in them.

'Sic your sheep dog on him,' Mister Spingler commanded Mister Toothill. 'I'll wager *he* can make him break from that trot.'

Israel Toothill made a hissing sound, and with a yelp the dog was off. Across the pasture he chased the colt, snapping and barking at his heels. But the colt danced neatly out of his way, never once shifting from his trot.

William Rysdyk broke out in a chuckle that made the blood rise in Mister Spingler's face. The little man spun around, turning his back on the sight. 'You, Rysdyk!' he said, coming very close to him. 'We've a challenge to propose to you.'

As William Rysdyk's head went up in surprise, his beard brushed Mister Spingler's long bill nose.

The man stepped back in disgust. 'We have come,' he sniffed, rubbing his nose, 'to propose for your beast a public trial at the Union Course on Long Island. This would give you an opportunity to show his speed. And *fairly,*' he added, 'with no umbrella to frighten his opponent.'

William Rysdyk stood with his mouth open, looking at the faces of the men, from one to the other. The import of the words numbed him. The Union Course. Long Island. A public trial. Over the same mile Bishop's Hambletonian and Silvertail had trotted!

'Well?' Mister Spingler said sharply.

'Excuse, sir. It fuddles me. What say you again?'

Mister Spingler felt his colleagues' eyes on him. He pulled himself up, speaking deliberately. 'Perhaps you are afraid. Afraid your horse lacks the stamina.'

'Him?' William Rysdyk exploded. 'Why, he can trot out quicker as a dog, sir, and he still got some power over. By golly, look on him now.'

Mister Spingler turned around to look. It was true. The colt with the dog yapping at his heels seemed as fresh as when he had pranced out of his stall.

'Please to call up your dog, sir,' William Rysdyk said, surprised at his own boldness.

When the dog came in, panting and slavering, John Doughty and Israel Toothill and Mister Dandy broke into the talk, anxious to get the matter settled. Their sentences came quick and staccato.

'The match will come off Tuesday next.'

'Sharp at three.'

'Trotting against your colt will be his half brother—Abdallah Chief, owned by Mister Roe.'

'First The Chief will trot the mile. Then your horse.'

'The better time wins.'

'As to the matter of finances,' the banker said, 'the committee will pay the costs of shipping your colt over the Erie, and Mister Seely has donated the use of his skeleton wagon, the same one Silvertail drew over the same course.'

Now everything was said. A strained silence followed, broken only by the panting of the sheep dog.

Mister Spingler tapped his boot, vexed at the delay. 'Do you or do you not wish to match him?' He fairly shouted the question.

'That I know not, sir. Abdallah Chief—him I have seen. He is over the four years, leaned from the racing. Hambletonian, he is yet a round-barreled colt, and only three times in the harness.'

'Very well, if you have no confidence . . .'

William Rysdyk gave a look of contempt. 'Who said it we would not go? We got to!' he announced, pride rising in him.

The banker pulled a notebook and a lead pencil from the tail of his coat. 'Now then, how do you spell your horse's name, Rysdyk?'

William Rysdyk began—slowly, haltingly. 'Hah, ah, em, bay, el, ay, tay, oh, en, ee, ah, en.'

Mister Spingler smiled down his nose. 'Gentlemen,' he said, 'the oaf has named the colt after our hero, Alexander Hamilton, yet he knows not how to spell the name.'

A deep flush came over William Rysdyk's face. How could he explain to the men that he had named his horse for Hambletonian, the hero of his childhood? He would not try.

The driver laughed. 'Why not call him Rysdyk's Big Bull? It will add flavor to the notices. Rysdyk's Big Bull against The Chief.'

148

11: Match Against Time

Tuesday next came, and William Rysdyk and Hambletonian were in New York City. Early that morning William Rysdyk stepped into a new jewelry store called Tiffany's.

'A timekeeper I would want to buy,' he said timidly to the spruce gentleman who leaned across the showcase. 'To click it on when my colt strikes off on the Union Course. What for time-keepers have you?'

The gentleman opened a narrow drawer behind him and took out a shiny watch on a long cord. 'Of course, you know how it works,' he said, 'but I should like to make certain it is in perfect order.' Turning the face toward William Rysdyk, he clicked the pin. He let the seconds run, sixty of them, and clicked it again. Then he placed the watch in his customer's hand, saying, 'In perfect condition!' Thus in his quiet, thoughtful way the jeweler had shown a frightened stranger in New York how to work a stop watch.

He smiled as he held open the door. 'Remember, time waits for neither man nor horse.'

'Is true!' William Rysdyk nodded heartily. He walked away, smiling to himself. 'That Mr. Tiffany will make a go of it, I betcha.'

His smile died on his lips. A light rain was falling. 'Ach, the track!' he cried, clapping his hands to his head. 'It goes sticky on me.' He was in a frenzy to get there, as if he could mop it up singlehanded.

But when he did get there, the rain was falling in a steady

curtain. There was nothing to do but watch it out the window of Hambletonian's stall. Desolated, he threw a blanket on the straw and lay down, inviting Hambletonian to join him. Together, man and colt slept, and the rain quieted and stopped, and the wind came up and blew a gale.

And as they slept, the first spectators began coming to the course, spreading handkerchiefs and butcher's paper over the damp seats. Jonas Seely left his group in the stands to look in on his hired man.

'Ho there, Rysdyk! Awake! The hour is at hand!'

William Rysdyk scrambled to his feet and looked up at the sky. 'The weather strikes around. God lets go the pump handle, eh?'

'Aye, but a gale blows now. However, it takes more than wind and storm to keep true sportsmen away. Naturally, the assemblage is not so great as it was for the race between Fashion and Peytona or for Fashion and Boston, but what it lacks in numbers it makes up in quality.'

'So?'

'Aye,' Mister Seely nodded. 'Already I have spotted Oliver Holmes, Ralph Emerson, and His Honor, Ambrose T. Kingsland, Mayor of New York.'

William Rysdyk came out of the stall and looked at the stands.

His mouth went dry. Top hats and poke bonnets were thick as flies in a blacksmith shop, and in the centerfield was a higgledy-piggledy conglomeration of carts and gigs and chariots and landaus and phaetons and broughams. He had never seen so many turnouts. He looked helplessly at Mister Seely.

'Excuse, sir, Hambletonian and me—is maybe better we tail it from here. We could home be already by morning.'

'Come, come, man. The colt will give you confidence. The gentleman yonder,' he indicated the direction with a slight lift of his elbow, 'the one smoking the big cigar, is Mister Roe, owner of Abdallah Chief.'

William Rysdyk took one look at the man, standing big and calm, watching while his hired help wheeled out one of the new sulkies. William Rysdyk wished he were at home. Digging ditches. Sacking onions. Splitting wood. Anything. If only he had known! Now it was too late. He looked down at the patches on his knees, at his stable boots.

The crowd was growing. Mister Seely pulled out his watch. 'Half after two,' he said. 'Note Mister Roe now. He is warming up The Chief. He trots the mile at three on the hour. Then immediately afterward comes your turn.'

With hands cold and trembling William Rysdyk began harnessing—slipping the collar over Hambletonian's head, his tail through the crupper, putting the pad on his back, buckling the bellyband.

As his hands touched the colt, he asked himself, 'What matters it if my breeches is rough and patched? Hambletonian's coat is satin, without flaw, his hoofs shining from beeswax. The crowd —they come for him, not me.'

Hambletonian was restive, sensing the tension in the air. Today there was no rattle of milk cans. Today was different. And the wind! Already it distended his nostrils, lifted his mane, excited him.

The bugles and drums! The wind had affected them, too. Quavered the notes, carried them high on wind shoulders.

Now Mister Roe was driving Abdallah Chief out on the track. How slim and sleek The Chief! How wiry from his racing! The spectators liked him. Their cheers left no doubt.

'The cheers care I not for!' said William Rysdyk, trying to believe his own words. 'What matters is the time.' He held his watch on The Chief.

'Go!' came the word. And The Chief went, hugging the rail, taking advantage of the distance saved. William Rysdyk's eyes darted ahead to the quarter pole, waiting for the horse to pass it. As he whipped by, the new watch said forty-four seconds!

The assemblage was on its feet. Abdallah Chief was going the pace they expected. One twenty-nine at the half. Now his pace was increasing. Two-eleven and a half at the three-quarter pole. Faster down the stretch! He was passing the wire now—two minutes, fifty-five and a half seconds at the finish.

The time was good in the gale, the crowd satisfied with its choice. Better marks had been made, they told each other. Flora

152

Temple had done the same distance in less time. So had Lady Suffolk. But then the track had been fast and the wind still. The performance of The Chief was good. Mister Roe drove him back to his stall, looking mightily pleased. The Chief, however, seemed tired on his legs, blowing as if his lungs were fit to burst.

Again the bugle shrilling in the wind. But if it had been no louder than a penny whistle it would have pierced William Rysdyk's ears. And now the roll of the drums. The bugle and the drums were in him, inside him, in his stomach, his lungs, his heart.

Now it was! Now the time had come! He mounted Silvertail's big wagon, set his feet against the dashboard, braced himself. He took the reins. He cradled the stop watch in his palm. To his surprise his hand held steady and it was the crowd that fluttered. What if their cheers were few and raveling away in laughter? His eyes and ears were not for them. He was seeing between the ears of his colt, seeing the wet, gummy mile, waiting for the word.

'Go!' it came like a knifeblade sharpened on the wind. The colt and the watch clicked off in unison. And suddenly William Rysdyk knew the watch was his opponent. Not The Chief, but the live little thing in his hand. The little gold thing with a white face and little fine wires inside. She was his opponent.

The sticky track was on her side, cupping at the colt's feet, sucking at them, holding them back. The high wind was on her side, blowing pieces of paper in Hambletonian's face. The white picket fence was on her side. The colt had never seen such a high fence before. He shied from it. No hugging the rail to save precious yards and seconds.

The seconds were ticking themselves off, ticking away all safe and secure, away from the wind, away from the fence, away from the cuppy track. Time was his match! Time grinning up at him from the white face with gimpy, nervous little hands.

In front of him the satin haunches, the driving legs punching out, clawing to grip the track, clawing and slipping. On the first turn the heavy wagon began to skewer. William Rysdyk slowed the piston legs, slowed them. Even the turns were on the watch's side.

Forty-one seconds at the quarter pole. The colt was a match for Time! Now for a half mile without any turns. And the colt knew it, going like a steam engine, his tail the black smoke. Now the wind was a prodding stick, pricking inside his nose, pricking along his chest, his barrel, his legs, lifting his forelock, his mane. Rushing at him on all sides, jangling in his ears, spurring him.

One twenty-three at the half! William Rysdyk felt pride rising with the wind. His colt was speed, harnessed speed.

Tears blurred his eyes. He blinked them fiercely away. Two-seven and a half at the third quarter. The horse and Time were flying together, beat for beat, second for second.

Now one more turn. The wagon sluing again on the wet clay, teetering on two wheels! William Rysdyk leaned far out to hold it on the track, pushing with his body, his feet, holding his breath in anguish as two iron tires spun free of the earth in a singing whine.

Too late now to slow down. He leaned harder, the breath hurting in his lungs. And then to his relief he felt the wagon settling down, felt the jolt and the relief all in one.

Now the brush down the stretch! William Rysdyk straining, pushing forward, sitting bird-light in the seat, longing to trot alongside the colt, yoked to him, somehow worthy of him.

The white face in his hand! Two minutes, forty-eight and a half seconds as they crossed the finish line. Hambletonian had won! His time was better than The Chief's! Seven seconds better!

The crowd was finding its voice, waving handkerchiefs and

muffs big as bedpillows. The crowd was a flag of many colors, flung on the wind, now rippling in, closing in on Hambletonian. And the judge was jumping down from his perch, raising his hand, shouting with the throng.

'Huzzah for Rysdyk's Big Bull! Huzzah for Rysdyk's Big Bull!'

Suddenly William Rysdyk's voice burst into a shout, lustier than any other: 'Hurrah for Rysdyk's Big Bull!'

The 'bull' himself stood shining with sweat, his ears laced back, not because he was displeased but because he was the son of Old Abdallah!

'Excuse, please.' William Rysdyk tried to speak out above the applause. 'The colt he must not stand in the wind. I must now walk him out and put his blanket on, walking him cool.' But his voice was lost in the huzzahs.

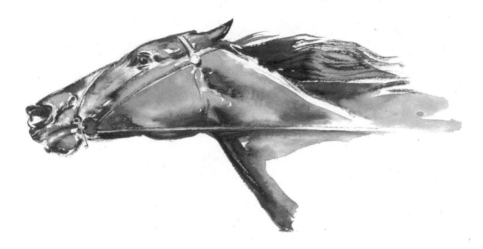

Nineteen

GIBSON leaned back against the pillows. The rain had stopped and a watery spot of sun filtered through the trees and found his bulletin board. It marked Alma Lee's picture—Alma Lee whom he had driven against time. In the shadowy fringes around the sun were Rosalind's pictures, Rosalind whose speed was still untried. He closed his eyes and dreamed the race of Rosalind. All of it. He saw himself in it. But mostly he saw Rosalind. Big-going like Hambletonian. Born to trot.

He opened his eyes and looked around the room, at Mike splashing water on a canvas and getting a tree instead of a puddle, at Grubber squinting his near-sighted eyes as he worked with a tiny spring on a freight-car wheel. Only Beaver was watching him hungrily.

"Say, Gib," he said, "I'm still waiting for that book. You memorizing it?"

"Only one little skinny chapter left, Beaver."

"Okay. But, jeepers creepers, I get all excited just looking at you."

The few pages had to wait for everyday things. When a quiet time came early next morning before breakfast, Gibson tried to read the words slowly to make them last. But they were quicksilver.

12: The Great Sire

Top hats, handkerchiefs, muffs were still waving over the Union Course as William Rysdyk drove off. The performance of the untried colt had first stunned and thrilled the spectators; then a wondering set in. What could Rysdyk's Big Bull have done with training? With a skilled driver? On a fast track? On a windless day? What could he have done hooked to a light sulky instead of a cumbrous wagon?

And now what could he, as a sire, do to improve the speed and stamina of the American trotter? The question flew from mouth to mouth during the weeks that followed the Union Course race. And more than one man stood ready to answer it. Stock-breeders, dirt farmers, dairymen, men cooped up in office buildings, men from near, men from far—all wanted to buy the colt. Two gentlemen journeyed up from Virginia to bid ten thousand dollars for him. At first their offers were spoken low, in quiet confidence, then their offers and voices were raised in impatience.

'Sh! Don't speak it so loud,' William Rysdyk would say, motioning toward Hambletonian. 'He don't like it. Already I know him since he was eating off his mare-mom. No, by criminy! Hambletonian and me—we wouldn't going to separate now. There's nobody could *buy* him.'

In the years that followed, many horsemen brought their mares to Hambletonian to be bred and thus improve their trotting stock. One was Ulysses S. Grant, President of the United States. It was the President's approval that helped carry the name of Hambletonian throughout the world.

And it was the President who noted a unique characteristic in Hambletonian's colts: their hips stood higher than their withers. He gave a name to this conformation. The "trotting pitch" he called it. And what Israel Toothill and his august committee had once laughed at, horsemen now began seeking.

With each year Hambletonian's fame grew and spread. At one Orange County Fair, while a vast throng sent up cheers and clamorings, Hambletonian and nine of his big-going sons trotted around a giant oak tree in the centerfield.

'Hero of Orange County! King of Sires!' they shouted now. And the name 'Rysdyk's Big Bull' buried itself in the dust of the past.

His son Bruno became the first four-year-old to trot the mile in 2:30; George Wilkes made a world record of 2:22; Jay Gould, 2:21½; Orange Girl, 2:20; Nettie, 2:18. And his son Dexter became a household word for speed. He won forty-seven out of fifty-one races, reducing the world record to 2:17¼. And it mattered not to the great Dexter whether he trotted in harness, to wagon, or under saddle. He won!

Good as these marks were, none stood. Hambletonian's grandchildren and great-grandchildren kicked their heels at them, setting up new marks of their own—2:11½ for St. Julien; 2:10 for Jay-Eye-See, 2:08¾ for Maud S.; 2:07 for Peter the Great.

The line strengthened as it lengthened! Each new generation clipped off seconds until Hambletonian became the most famous stallion in all America.

Year on year at the county fairs, old and young would stop in admiration when William Rysdyk drove him into the grounds. And year on year the stallion would win blue ribbons with gold lettering that said, 'Best stallion in his class.' He won silver cups, too, and a sterling silver tea set because of all stallions he was the best.

Of course, William Rysdyk had no more use for silver cups and tea sets than for water in his hat, but he accepted them all as custodian for Hambletonian. And often on moon-bright nights he would steal out to the barn with lye ashes and rag to polish them. 'Foolish, eh?' he would chortle as he rubbed. 'Yah, foolish but not caring. In some other world maybe his thirst gets gentler and out of tea cups he drinks.'

In time William Rysdyk's beard turned white, and white hairs too grew around Hambletonian's muzzle. And still the horse was above price. As the man and the stallion grew old together, they looked upon each other with their hearts as well as their eyes.

One early spring evening shortly before his death, William Rysdyk motioned to the youngest Seely boy, man-grown now, who sat in his room tending him. The young man got up and knelt beside the bed, looking into the bearded face and the pleading eyes.

'There is two wishes I could maybe want to wish.' William Rysdyk's breath came short but a smile played about his lips. 'Can you once to boost up on me so out my window Hambletonian I could see?'

With awkward but gentle hands the young man propped the pillows behind the hired man's back. Then he threw wide the shutters, saying, 'I will go out now and lead your horse in front of the window.'

Turning to leave the room, something caused him to look back. To his wonderment he saw the stallion footing his way slowly and majestically toward the open window. Head upraised, ears

161

pricked forward like trumpets, he came closer, step by step. He may only have been harkening to the cry of a hawk thin on the wind, but perchance he heard a beloved voice calling. As his head reached the window, the voice spoke only two words. 'Till seeing,' it said, 'till seeing.'

At sound of the familiar singsong the stallion began to quiver, and suddenly in a long trembling neigh of remembrances added his voice to One Man's.

With a sigh of satisfaction William Rysdyk sank back among the pillows. 'When deep sleep comes to him,' he whispered to the Seely boy, 'he has it on the green hillside with a name marker? Yah? In my will we make it up so? Yah?'

The young man nodded.

And so it was.

It is not given to horses to write wills. But some there are who say Hambletonian's descendants are his testament.

And some say Hambletonian wrote his will in music—American music, the tap-tap, tap-tap ringing of hoofbeats.

Gibson turned the page and was about to close the book when his eye fell upon a pocket pasted inside the back cover. Edging out of it, a piece of notepaper was plainly visible. At first he thought it might be a family letter belonging to Dr. Mills. Then he spied the top of a "G" and the top of a "b,"

and the more he looked the more he felt the two letters might be part of his own name.

He pulled the paper out of the pocket a little, and then a little more, and suddenly he was reading Dr. Mills' scrawling handwriting.

Dear Gib,

Hambletonian does have a big-marked tombstone. But I like to think that the world's premier trotting race, the Hambletonian, is his real monument, a living one. And it seems just right that each year the race is held in Goshen, Orange County, an easy trot from the little knoll where the horse was born.

Each August when I see the field come pounding down the stretch, I like to remember that America originated harness racing. Horse racing may be the sport of kings, but harness racing belongs to the American people. To England the Thoroughbred, to France the Percheron, to America the Trotter.

And I like knowing that America owes her trotting breed to a bearded countryman who saw greatness in an awkward colt whose dam was a cripple and whose sire was mule-eared and ugly. Nearly all trotters today owe their pure gait and pluck to the blood of Rysdyk's Hambletonian.

I hope your Rosalind will race in the Hambletonian. Whether she wins or not, I'd like to see her pay this tribute to One Man's Horse.

And now, Gib, the book is yours. To keep for your own. I'm quite sure my grandfather would be glad it now belongs to someone with staying power and gameness not unlike the son of Old Abdallah.

Doc Mills

Twenty

GIBSON looked at the letter a long time before he folded it and slid it into its pocket. He closed the book gently, turned the key and left it in the lock. He got up then and put on his bathrobe and slippers. The other boys were still asleep. Leaving the book on Beaver's table, he tiptoed out of the room.

At the east end of the cottage, past the warming kitchen and the telephone booth, was a sunroom where visitors could wait while a patient finished his bath or nap. Now there was no one in the room. Only wicker chairs and a table, and ivy plants outgrowing their pots. Green window shades were partly drawn, leaving a strip of brightness across the floor. Gibson paced up and down within it, being careful not to step on the line at the edge of the sun. It reminded him of the way he hopped over the cracks in the sidewalk when he was little. With the book ended he felt as young as that. Young and alone and suddenly bereft.

"What is it I want?" he asked himself as he padded duck-footed up and down, knotting and unknotting his belt. His voice gave no answer, but he knew what was the matter. It was the terrible longing in him. The longing to see his own horse, to be to her what Rysdyk had been to Hambletonian, to hold the reins over her and to know she knew who it was telegraphing to her. It was no longer enough to live on another man's dreams. No longer enough to live on the border of his own.

"Oh, here you are, Gib!" It was Tante. "I've been hunting all over the place for you. Here are two registered packages. They both came special delivery. Look legal and important, don't they?" She handed Gibson two brown envelopes with big blotches of red sealing wax along the flaps. Then taking a pencil from the twist of hair on top of her head, she pointed to her open receipt book. "Sign here, please."

She started to leave, then came back. "I'm an early bird, too," she winked. "I'll not tell that I found you up before breakfast."

Alone again, Gibson looked at the envelopes. They were both addressed in his father's hand and both postmarked the same day but at different hours. He would open the earlier one first.

A strange excitement seized him as he broke the seal and took out a parchment-like paper. He spread it on the table between fingertips that began to tremble. It was—at long last—Rosalind's certificate! He remembered seeing others like it hanging in the polished offices of big horse owners. But there they were just something in a frame. Unexciting. Like a banked fire instead of a blazing one.

He read in a whisper the important words.

ROSALIND, bay mare, bred by BENJAMIN FRANKLIN WHITE; passed to GIBSON B. WHITE.

The letters stood out so sharply he half expected them to be raised, like letters chiseled on stone. His finger traced them.

"This is to certify," the words marched on, "that ROSALIND has been duly registered in the American Trotting Register and her pedigree therein can be traced."

Gibson held the document at arm's length. It was the most exciting piece of paper he had ever looked at. In the upper left a symbol of a horse in full trot almost flew off the page; in the

lower left a red seal shone like a small sun. And all around the margin, as if to box in the wonder and excitement, was a curlicue of green like some old, old frame. And the letters at the top of the page looked old, too, like the chapter titles in *One Man's Horse*.

Gingerly he laid the document down and turned now to the second envelope. Within it were two papers, one folded like a road map. A brief note was attached.

Dear Gib,

Rosalind's pedigree at last! It'd take a piece of paper five feet square to hold all of the families in her ancestry, so this isn't as extended as it could be. But even so, your mother and I've been burning a lot of midnight oil to get it done. So many letters had to be written, checking and double checking.

Rosalind's pedigree is yours to keep. The other paper is invaluable and has been loaned to me by my friend Dick Miller of Orange County. We used to picnic on his hilltop when you were a small boy. Remember? Mrs. Miller always made ginger-bread for you.

Yours,

Dad

P.S. Rosalind is training on. We think she'll live up to the pride of her birth.

Gibson unfolded the pedigree. And there, in his mother's best handwriting, was Rosalind's family tree, with so many roots it took his breath.

He began reading the names, smiling to himself, yet almost afraid to smile. Suppose the names did not build up to the one name! "Rosalind by Scotland," he began, "he by Peter

Scott, he by Peter the Great." Suddenly he stopped, holding his forefinger on Peter the Great. His eye sneaked on ahead and now his voice was catching up. "Peter the Great by Pilot Medium, he by Happy Medium, he by—Rysdyk's Hambletonian!"

There it was! Rosalind a direct descendant!

A direct descendant of Rysdyk's Hambletonian! For a horse, it was like coming over on the Mayflower!

This was too good to keep. Even Mike and Beaver and Grubber would be excited about it. He started to leave, folding the pedigree, returning it to its envelope, then saw the other paper his father had mentioned. It was littler and older looking, fuzzed up by age.

With a sigh he took it out. This had to be an anti-climax. One day's mail could not possibly hold more excitement. But as his eye caught the heading, his heart stood still. Emblazoned across the sheet was the pedigree of Hambletonian himself!

HAMBLETONIAN by ABDALLAH

𝕻edigree: Hambletonian was sired by Old Abdallah, he by Mambrino, he by Imported Messenger. His dam was the Charles Kent Mare by Imported Bellfounder, granddam old One Eye, by Bishop's Hambletonian, and he by Imported Messenger, and his dam also by Imported Messenger.

Gibson read the names again. They rang in his ears, flashed pictures in his mind. Messenger charging down the gangplank with grooms swinging from his lead ropes like monkeys on a vine; a limping mare pulling a butcher's cart; a big-going colt flying around the Union Course against wind and time.

Old Abdallah. Bishop's Hambletonian. The Kent Mare. Messenger. He mouthed the names. He was better than Aladdin! He didn't need a magic lamp. He could rub his tongue over the words and the pictures came. Just like that.

With quick, careful fingers he returned each document to its envelope. Then he flew down the hall, slippers flapping.

"Fellows," he shouted, "Wake up! Listen to this. Rosalind was by Scotland, he by Peter Scott, he by Peter the Great. Peter the Great by Pilot Medium, he by Happy Medium, he by Rysdyk's Hambletonian!"

"Sounds like the begats in the Bible," said Mike, turning over in bed and reaching for an orange.

"Looks like your filly could be a D. A. R.," Beaver yawned.

"For a horse she could! Her forefathers came over with Messenger. It's like landing with the Pilgrims. Why, she's as American as Priscilla and John Alden. I can go on with her pedigree on her dam's side, too."

"Oh—no!" Mike put in. "Here, catch." He threw an orange at Gibson. Gibson caught it but did not eat. He was busy at his bulletin board, rearranging all the pictures to make room.

Rosalind 1:56¾
{
  Scotland 1:59¼
  {
    Peter Scott 2:05 { Peter the Great 2:07¼ { Pilot Medium { Happy Medium 2:04 { RYSDYK'S HAMBLETONIAN ; Santos } } ; Jenny Scott 2:14¼ }
    Roya McKinney 2:07½
  }
  Alma Lee 2:04¾
  {
    Lee Worthy 2:02½ { Lee Axworthy 1:58¼ }
    Jane Revere 2:06¾ { Guy Axworthy 2:08¾ { Peter the great 2:07¼ { Pilot Medium { Happy M. 2:04 { RYSDYK'S HAMBLETONIAN } } ; Nervolo Belle } } ; Volga 2:04½ }
  }
}

Twenty-One

THE hours flowed over the little cottage in the Cumberlands in torrents and in dribbles. Eat. Sleep. Footsteps coming. Footsteps going. Games by lamplight. Then alone in bed in the dark. And each heart pinching, wondering who would be the first to strike out for home.

The days fell away, and the months. A year wore itself out. And now Gibson's letters from his father were shorter but the words bigger.

FROM LEXINGTON, JUNE 1

Rosalind and I are starting out on the Grand Circuit. Nobody very high on her now but her owner and trainer.

FROM CLEVELAND, JUNE 20

Rosalind's got it! Got everything we ever thought she had. Maybe more. She just won the Rainy Day Sweepstakes. Never skipped a beat.

FROM GOSHEN, JULY 5

Rosalind did it again! Took the Good Time Stake for two-year-olds. Finished flying.

FROM LEXINGTON, OCTOBER 10

Rosalind just set a new record in the Junior Kentucky Futurity. Chalked up the fastest quarter and half mile for her age. Her competition was Ed Lasater, but she led all the way home. Time 2:03.

As Rosalind improved, Gibson improved. Each letter brought a dosage of strength with it.

"You'll be lighting out soon," Mike predicted. "I can tell by your look when you come in from walking about the grounds. I've seen it before."

"Yeh," Beaver said. "I've seen it, too. A contented look like an old moo cow who knows where her next meal is coming from."

Grubber nodded. "I better start making him a caboose to take along for his grandchildren."

"And I better finish that drawing of Rosalind," Mike put in. "Some day, we'll read in the papers about the famous young driver winning with Rosalind. And we'll say, 'Shucks, we knew the kid way back when he hadn't a shirt to his back, only a pair of pajamas.'"

Beaver sighed. "Some day they'll just come in and tell him to clear out. And then the sheets'll be changed and a new guy'll come in."

The predictions came startlingly true. One early spring day without any warning, without any fanfare. Dr. Mills was pacing up and down in the room like a lion in a cage too small.

He stopped suddenly, spinning around to look full at Gibson. "Start packing, boy," he smiled. "It's time to leave the nest."

171

No one in the room said anything. Beaver's ruler fell to the floor. A bird landed on the eavestrough and began hopping with wiry feet.

"What?" the voice quavered.

Dr. Mills nodded as if he didn't trust his own voice.

Now Gibson was out of bed, clutching Dr. Mills' arm. "For good?"

"For good, if—" Dr. Mills' laugh was deep but his look earnest, "if you stay well within yourself. If you don't try to be race horse, polo pony, and hunter all in one."

Gibson let go the doctor's arm and sat down on the edge of the bed. "I won't!" he cried, and the joy in him was so sharp it was like a sense of pain.

"Your father is coming on the noon train. You can leave with him."

"Dad knows?"

"He knows."

Gibson just sat there, stunned at the suddenness.

"He doesn't want to leave, fellows." Dr. Mills spoke to the other boys. "Likes your company too much."

Gibson made no move to get up. His eyes went from Dr. Mills to the floor. He shuffled his feet in and out of his slippers. "Something I've got to ask," he stammered. "Something—"

"Want to come out to the sunroom?"

"No, sir. Mike and Beaver and Grubber are my friends. I can take it in front of them. Dr. Mills—?"

"Yes, Gib."

Gibson couldn't speak for a little while and when he did, his voice came out thin and stringy. "The Hambletonian race," he said. "It's coming up."

"Yes, I know. August twelfth."

172

Dr. Mills waited for the question to come. When Gibson didn't ask it, he turned to speak quietly to the room in general. "It's kind of comforting to know other fellows besides myself have problems." Then he went to Mike's bed. "Is Rosalind declared in?" he asked, looking at the painting of her.

"Yes, sir." Gibson followed and stood beside Dr. Mills, looking at the painting too. Looking, but not seeing. "Doc?" his next words came hard spoken. "Could I—that is, could I drive her in the race?"

This time it was Dr. Mills who was straining for the right words, trying to be boy and doctor both. "It all depends, Gib," he said at last.

"Depends on what?"

"On things so simple they're hard to do."

"Just name 'em, Doc."

"No, Gib. You name them. Two words'll do it. And no prompting, please, from the audience."

Gibson relaxed. "Rest?" he asked.

"That's the first word, Gib. Sleep if you can, every blessed afternoon. But if you can't sleep, just rest."

The boy nodded. "Could 'eat' be the second word? The feed bag at regular intervals?"

Dr. Mills smiled, remembering back to the day in his office when he had first seen Gibson. "For a second time you've written the right prescription."

"Then you mean—it's all right with you—if I drive in the Hambletonian? Can I, Doc?"

"Seems to me that's up to the judgment of her trainer and the strength of her owner. If the trainer and owner agree—"

"You mean—it's all right with you?"

"Why not?"

173

Why not! Why not! The words charged the room, filled the room, spilled out the window. Sang themselves to the whole world.

"The final prep for a colt is about four months, isn't it?" Dr. Mills asked.

"Yes, sir."

"That should be enough for you, too. Boys are not much slower than colts. See here, Gib, will you pack or do we have to do it for you?"

"I'll do it!" Now Gibson was alive—stumbling across the room, picking up Beaver's ruler, handing it to him, opening the closet door, coming out again with his grip.

"Better put on some clothes first, young fellow. And how about saying good-by? I'll be leaving before you do."

"Leaving? Where to, Doc?"

"For Canada. Trout fishing. Some of us doctors have chartered a plane. It's a trim red-and-white craft with a top wing."

As Gibson shook the big hand held out to him, he couldn't help noticing the palm and the fingertips. Neither hard nor soft, but like the big pads of a St. Bernard dog that had footed many miles on errands of mercy.

"Good-by, Gib."

"Good-by—and oh, thanks, Doc."

Dr. Mills shook hands with Mike and Beaver and Grubber. "When I get back from Canada," he said to them, "you fellows should be ready to leave."

At the door he stopped. "And, Gib, I hope to fly down to Goshen for the Hambletonian. Seldom miss it. Last year I saw Greyhound set a record of two-two and a quarter. Your filly will have to go some to beat that."

Twenty-Two

GIBSON made his hands and legs go from bed to dresser and back again without doing handsprings. He emptied the drawer of pajamas onto the bed. Paisley pajamas. Striped pajamas. Polka dots. He'd seen enough pajamas to last him the rest of his days. He caught himself whistling a gay tune, then thought of the other boys and stopped.

"Hey, Gib, let me pack for you." It was Beaver talking. "You're as awkward as a pup in a grab bag." He pushed Gibson aside. "You tend to your saddlebags and bulletin board. We'll take care of the rest."

It took all hands to pack. And something of each boy went into the packing.

"You can have this picture of Rosalind," Mike offered.

Gibson held it at arm's length. "It's good. You've got a nice sweaty gleam on her. Thanks, Mike." Covering it over very carefully with a shirt, he tied it with a pajama string.

"Here's that caboose for your grandchildren," Grubber said. "It's even got a working brake assembly underneath. I'll pack it in your bedroom slipper for safety. Gosh," he added, "if I'd known the size of your slipper, I could have made a whole train for you. Want a few more?"

"Heck, no. I'm not going to have that many grandchildren."

Beaver stood thinking. "I haven't anything to give you, Gib. Except . . ." His face lighted with a sudden idea. He rummaged around in his table drawer and came up with a rabbit's foot. "Except this!" he said, laying the brown-and-white paw in Gibson's hand.

At last Gibson was ready. Everything done. Saddlebags buckled. Snapshots and documents packed in a shoe box. Clothes bulging in a grip and Mike's picture on its side, making a lean-to against it.

The room that had been all bustle and stir suddenly went quiet. An emptiness had already come into it. The bulletin board gaped bare like a raw scar on a tree just torn by a storm.

The round-faced clock gone, its ticking silenced. Now the quiet. The stiff-faced smiles. The fixed looks. The trying to make talk.

When Mr. White burst into the room, carrying his driving silks over his arm, all four boys looked to him in relief.

"Beaver! Grubber! Mike!" he said with a warming smile for each.

Then he and Gibson were facing each other, the father's arms held wide to clasp the boy in them. They both made a movement forward, then both stopped. A glance of understanding shuttled between them. Gibson was almost a man, taller now than his father. They shook hands, each telegraphing his message of happiness. The slow years worn away. Everything right at last.

Now the words flew.

"Son! You've grown like a stalk of corn. You must be pushing six feet."

"No, Dad. Only five eleven and a half."

Mr. White laughed until he had all of the boys laughing with him. "Only five eleven and a half!"

His gaze darted over the room, to the empty bulletin board, to the saddlebags strapped and buckled, to the grip closed and waiting. Carefully he laid his driving silks over the foot of Gibson's bed. "Our train doesn't leave for an hour," he said, settling himself comfortably in a chair.

Gibson grinned. Wherever his father sat he suddenly belonged. On a hilltop, on a fence rail, in a stable, in a hospital— he was like his old pork-pie hat. At home anywhere.

"Maybe," he was saying in his comfortable voice, "maybe your roommates would be interested in the news about your filly."

Beaver passed a plate of fruit to Mr. White. "We sure would," he said. "We know her pretty well, too."

Mr. White selected a banana. "Rosalind," he began, enjoying this moment to the full, "is entered in the Hambletonian."

The boys exchanged smiles.

"I've told them, Dad. They've known it for days."

"That's only half the news," his father went on, emphasizing his words with the banana.

Gibson didn't see how the day could possibly hold any more news without bursting at the seams. He watched his father get up and put the banana on top of the luggage. "This'll taste good on the train," he said. "Always like to eat and look out the window. Ever since I was a boy, journeys and bananas have gone together."

"What's the other half of the news, Dad?" Gibson asked anxiously.

Mr. White took a deep breath. "Well," he said, giving each boy a smile, "I was supposed to drive Ed Lasater for Mr. Reynolds in the Hambletonian, but do you know what he's done?"

"No. What?" asked Gibson, wondering whether his father meant the man or the horse.

"Well, he's released me."

"Released you!" Gibson's heart began to pound. He had an inkling of what was coming, could see it ahead like a red warning in the dark. He tried to make his voice sound steady, but it went high like a girl's. "Released you from what?"

"From driving Ed Lasater. You see, Mr. Reynolds knew I'd bred and trained Rosalind and watched over her like a baby, and, well—that's the kind of man Mr. Reynolds is." He stood up now, grinning. "I've just bought some new racing silks so Rosalind's owner will be proud of his driver as well as his filly. Brought 'em along," he said to Gibson, "thinking your roommates'd like to see them, too. By George," he laughed, "I'll have to keep them folded in my trunk for months, like a girl with a hope chest."

Mr. White's step had as much spring to it as a boy's. He went over to the bed and took off his coat. Then he shook the folds out of the new jacket and slipped it on. He squared the cap on his head. "Some folks think," he said as he buttoned the jacket and fastened the belt, "that black with white trimmings is too sober. But I've always felt the horse's coat should take the eye first. Not the driver's."

He looked at himself in the mirror over the empty dresser. "Maybe I'm getting old," he chuckled, "but a right smart horse in front of me can make up for a lot of years."

He turned around, facing the boys. "Like it?" he asked, his eyes young and lively.

Grubber and Beaver said, "It's fine."

Mr. White sighed happily, as if the long years of worry were over and everything was shaping up at last.

Mike said, "Gib, tell your dad what the doctor told you."

In the listening stillness Gibson suddenly felt very old. His voice, too, sounded old in his throat. "Dr. Mills said he was coming to see the Hambletonian."

"Say! That's wonderful!" Mr. White took off his cap and laid it on the bed. "Dr. Mills and Mr. Reynolds are about as good friends as a man and boy could have."

Now Mike was urging. "Tell him the rest, Gib. Tell him you're okay—tell him you can . . . "

Gibson silenced Mike with his looking. "Oh, yes," he

spoke as if suddenly remembering, "Mike wants me to tell you Dr. Mills said I'm out for good—if I stay well within myself."

"We'll see to that," Mr. White said, folding the coat in its original creases. "No driving until next winter down in Florida. Then one day you'll be in the Hambletonian yourself, clucking and crooning to a colt of Rosalind's."

Gibson got to his feet. He wanted to run away where no one could see him. There *was* a limit to the good news a day could hold. All at once it exploded and splattered back at you. He heard his father's voice.

"Anything the matter, Son?"

And his own voice answered, "No, Dad."

"You don't seem pleased at all the good news."

"I am, Dad. It's just that—"

Beaver came to the rescue. "Just too much excitement for one day," he suggested.

"That's it, Dad. Too much for one day." He moved toward the door. "I'll be right back," he said, trying to make his voice sound light, "I just want to say good-by to Tante and some of the nurses."

He went out of the room. He wanted to hide away from everyone. He headed for the sunroom, but even before he saw a figure pacing in the oblong of light, he heard a drone of voices. Now a nurse with some visitors in tow was coming toward him. He turned and dove into the telephone booth, closing the door behind him. He sat down on the small stool, and there in the little encompassing place, his pent-up feelings burst. Dry sobs shook him, wrenching from deep within.

How many times he had telephoned his father from this very booth! How many times he had picked up this receiver to hear the words, "Stay a little longer, Son. Everything'll work out. You'll see." The voice had often been tired, not matching the cheer of the words. But today his father was excited as any boy. He wanted to drive the colt he had bred and trained.

Gibson leaned his head against the hard mouthpiece and let the hot tears come. Out of the confusion of his mind he saw the gallant courage of his father. The eating in dingy restaurants, the sleeping in hot little rooming houses on the Grand Circuit. The fewer cigars. The old worn silks. The pinching and scraping and doing without to pay hospital bills. And all the while Rosalind his mainstay, his ray of hope. Rosalind whom he had bred. Rosalind whose ancestors he had marked. His father's words came to him: "The trainer is the wind. He blows upon the sapling colt, bending it in the way he wants it to grow."

"He's got to drive her!" The cry tore from him.

For a long time he sat in the little booth while his sobs grew quieter and farther apart. Then he knuckled the tears away and, unburdened at last, opened the door and went out.

In the cab on the way to the station, he said to his father, "It's good that Mr. Reynolds released you, Dad. You're the best driver I know."

A hand reached over and gripped his knee, and after a while a voice said, "Son, it's you who'll drive Rosalind in the Hambletonian. Don't you know a father'd rather see his son win than win himself?"

The hand was withdrawn in an impatient gesture. "That Doc Mills!" the voice exploded. "Why in thunderation didn't he tell *me* you could drive!"

"Who did tell you, Dad?"

"Nobody, really. I just got out my pry pole and pried it out

181

of those boys little by little, without their knowing. Any don-
derhead could tell something was wrong with the whole passel
of you."

"But, Dad—the new silks and all."

"Shucks, I've been needing new silks for a long time. Your
mother's been at me like a robin tugging a worm. Finally I
just gave in."

Gibson expelled a great lungful of air. "Then, you *want
me* to drive? You're glad?"

The car jolted to a sudden stop at the station. "By Jove,
Son, Rosalind understands English better than you do. You
can ask more fool questions than a four-year-old!"

"You mean it?"

Mr. White could see that the boy needed reassuring. He
spoke seriously now. "When the doctor says you can drive,
Gib, he says you are *well!* Do I mean it when I say I'm glad?
Boy, oh boy, do I mean it!"

He grabbed the heavy suitcase. "Come on, let's go! The
train's coming."

Twenty-Three

AT first glance the stables in Lexington seemed to Gibson unchanged, as if he had been away only days instead of years. Bear was there, wagging his stub tail and taking up with Gibson just where he had left off. And Guy Heasley hopping about spry-legged as ever. And the grooms sloshing leg bandages up and down in the suds. Only the faces that looked out of the stalls were different.

Gibson stood in the wide entrance of the stable and suddenly he became afraid. Afraid to look to right or left. What if Rosalind didn't live up to the promise of her pictures? What if she looked just like any other horse and he were to pass her by, still looking? He backed out, hesitating, stung by a moment's shame. Then he made himself go forward, across the sill and through the wide door. He felt rather than knew it was his father behind him, ready to come at a word or ready to disappear, leaving him alone in the tunnel of the barn.

Any other time Bear would have sensed Gibson's destination and sniffed on ahead, but now he remained at heel, patiently waiting the boy's next move.

Then all in a moment Gibson saw her. In the third stall on the left. He knew so unmistakably it was Rosalind that he walked straight toward her, never a look at the other heads straining curiously at him. He knew her, even though the little round colt look was gone and in its place an air of nobility. How did he know? He wondered himself. It was like meeting an old, old friend at a railroad station—your father, perhaps. As you watched the stream of people walking up the concourse from the train, you didn't have to say to yourself: one man among them will have a springiness in his walk and his eyes will be darkling blue and he'll be wearing an old pork pie hat and hunting you with a smile. You just looked. And suddenly there he was. Unlike all the others.

Just that quickly Gibson knew Rosalind. Among twenty heads there was hers. Rosalind stopping in the midst of grinding a bundle of hay, looking at him with the hay still wisped out like handlebar moustaches. For a long time she stood motionless, looking, not eating, then the wisps of hay began to teeter-totter, and then they were gone.

Slowly, with trembling fingers, Gibson unbolted the door of her stall, and he and Bear went inside with her. And Rosalind was bending her head down so Bear could curl his tongue across her muzzle and she was fluting her nostrils and lipping him. But for Gibson she had only a look of wariness.

His hand wanted to reach out to her, to stroke her neck

184

gently as if in the mere touching she might come to be his. But he stayed the impulse, knowing the touch would be more to comfort himself than her. He stood quiet, flattening himself against the planks of the stall, waiting.

He had no oats to offer, no sugar. He wanted no cupboard love from Rosalind. She was no pet, no plaything. She was a magnificent creature of bone and brawn and satin, with years of trotting music bred in her. He wanted her only to accept him as part of the sights and sounds and smells of her life, to go on about her business aware of him but not wary.

His eyes searched hers. Purple brown they were, with depths he could not plumb. And underlying the satin of her skin the network of veins ran like swollen rivers, and then branched out into threadlike tributaries. Some might say her tail was no plume of beauty, but it was long enough for a fly switch, and what else were tails for? *What else?*

He smiled as she turned toward the hayrack and pulled out more hay. By that small gesture, she had let him come into her world. And in that moment she had rolled the hospital years away. Gibson was back with the trotters! Back home where he belonged. Living again. Living ahead. Only four months to tune Rosalind for the Hambletonian. Only four months!

Gibson knew he had never been so happy. He made little trips into the woods for fresh green twigs. "Best kind of spring tonic for horses," Guy Heasley agreed as they both watched Rosalind strip the tender bark and eat it as if she'd had a special hankering for the bitter-sweet taste.

From the very beginning Gibson was allowed to spend the full morning at the track. "You be a railbird a while," his father told him. "Then look out! One day you'll be holding the reins over Rosalind."

And that was the way it happened. Appearing all of a sudden before him one day was Rosalind in harness, aloof and magnificent. And Guy Heasley was handing him the lines, grinning as if he, himself, had made this moment and the bigness of it. "Gib! Take over. It's one trip around at a slow jog. Orders from the boss."

And then Gibson was in the sulky seat, and once again he was going the wrong way of the track because he was only jogging. But the wrong way was the right way with Rosalind!

She was the biggest-going horse he'd ever seen. Alma Lee and Rocco seemed ponies by comparison. Yet her bigness was all rhythm and grace. For Gibson no one else on the track existed. He neither saw nor heard them. For him there were the two white feet and the two dark feet ticking in unison, like some highly wrought timepiece. And for him the electric touch of the reins, like twin messengers to her silk mouth.

Blood beating in his temples, he memorized her way of going, memorized everything about her. Her ears never still— forking this way, that way, pulling in sounds up ahead, sounds from behind. Against the sky they were not small, but he liked them as they were. Nice and big and friendly. You could tell how she felt about things.

187

He had to laugh at himself. He was just like William Rysdyk. Nothing wrong about his horse. Nothing. Her quarters, her hocks, her stride, her ears. Everything right. Exactly right.

And then in a wink the mile was over. That was all he could do. But it was a start, and the way was cut out for him.

Each morning now he jogged Rosalind before her workout. Each afternoon he slept in her stall. The straw bed was somewhat lumpy and somewhat prickly, but it was the best kind of cushion for sleeping and dreaming. Bear slipped into the stall too, snuggling himself into the hollow of Gibson's shoulder, snoring softly down his neck. Rosalind, however, dozed in quiet dignity, her neck arched and crested as she delicately balanced her nose in the straw.

As Gibson felt the squirming warmth of Bear and studied the beauty of Rosalind, he murmured Rysdyk's words, *"By golly, it ain't only one kind of joy, it's two!"* Then he fell asleep to the drony songs of the grooms as they cleaned harness in the alley in front of the stall.

By the middle of May Gibson was driving Rosalind both ways of the track.

By June he was working her, holding the stop watch on her, helping prepare her for the Grand Circuit.

By July he was on the Grand Circuit, watching her go her first race as a three-year-old. The day was July second. The town, North Randall, Ohio. He knew he would remember both always. For something happened to him there as he stood at the rail watching his father and Rosalind race together.

There was something grand and majestic about their togetherness. Gibson suddenly felt himself an onlooker, seeing things as they really were. Rosalind and his father a matched pair. It was the teamwork that made them great. The speed in his father's mind flowed through his hands into her mind. The two seemed even to think alike, often starting a heat with one plan, ending up with another.

For Gibson the race itself became a three-act play, gathering speed with each act, working up to the climax. He watch-timed the first heat in 2:06, the second in 2:05, the third in 2:04, with Rosalind going the last quarter in 29$\frac{2}{5}$ seconds to keep ahead of Ed Lasater. But it wasn't the fury of time that struck Gibson, and it wasn't the way the announcer paired the driver and horse—"Ladies and gentlemen, we congratulate *the grand master of the turf and his flying filly*"—it was the knowing that in her own eyes Rosalind belonged to his father. Always she would make the supreme effort for the hands and voice she knew so well.

There at North Randall, with the hot July sun beating down on him and friends reaching out to congratulate him on the performance of his filly, Gibson suddenly knew she was not really his at all. But, strangely, he didn't feel desolated in the least. He felt good and warm inside, as if the sun were within and without. A few years ago, or even a few months, he would have gone off like a hurt pup to whimper behind the barn because a bigger dog had taken his bone. But here he was, smiling and shaking hands, with a pride rising in him, pride for his father and for his filly both.

Morning found him trying to tell his father. It was dawn and they were both up and dressing in a little hotel room near the North Randall track.

"Dad," Gibson began as he daubed wax on his boots, "a filly like Rosalind wants to win her races, doesn't she?"

In front of the washstand mirror Mr. White tilted his head to scrape the stubble from his chin. He mumbled an unintelligible answer.

Gibson went on. "We've got to give her every chance to win the Hambletonian, haven't we?" He paused, watching the hand with the razor sweep down, jerk up, sweep down. Then, "Will you drive her for me, Dad?"

Mr. White kept on looking into the mirror, not at himself now but in the corner of the mirror at Gibson's face. With his eyes fixed on the boy, he held the washcloth under the hot water for a long time, then he twisted the water out and pressed it against his face, trying to give himself time to think, reaching for big words to answer the bigness of his son's understanding. But only puny words came.

"You're not feeling well?"

Gibson's eyes did not break away. "Never better, Dad." His calm tone astonished himself. Yesterday it had been easy to think these things, today it was easy to say them. He was explaining now as if his father were the boy. "You see, Dad, I know what it means to want to win. I don't want Rosalind ever to have the heart taken out of her by a driver who didn't understand her." He bent to his boots, polishing hard for a moment, then went on almost eagerly. "I'm still a stranger to her, you know. But for you she'll make the supreme effort. In fairness to her you've *got* to drive."

The father wiped his face dry and reached up and turned off the light over the mirror. He put on his shirt and tied his plain black tie and pulled up his suspenders over his shoulders.

"Yes," he said shyly, "I see what you mean." He went to the window and saw the sun tipping above the horizon. "You know, Gib, there are times when it's easy to make a prayer."

Twenty-Four

ALL that month of July Rosalind showed fast in her preparation for the Hambletonian. Like some prima donna who smiles on her prop man, she let Gibson help in the tuning up. Handling easy as you please, she let him take her two trips around the track, warming her up, limbering her up, getting her ready. Then his father would mount the sulky, and her muscles would quicken and she would gather herself and the two would set sail, effortlessly, like wind runneling along the grass.

The railbirds, holding watches on them, began to hum like a hive of bees.

"Something must've happened to my second hand!"

"I was about to say the same thing!"

"That filly must be part bird!"

"Now if I could find one like that I'd buy her on the spot."
"Why, she's having as much fun as Ben himself!"

By the end of July the railbirds were not alone in their thinking. The entire harness world had become aware of Rosalind. Here was a filly that had won the Junior Kentucky Futurity, the Good Time Stake, the Rainy Day Sweepstakes, the three-year-old Inaugural. A filly that had started seven times and won seven times!

Now, just two weeks before the great race, there was only one start left in her final preparation. The National at Old Orchard Beach, Maine, was called the dress rehearsal of the Hambletonian. History had made a glib phrase about it and had rammed it down the throats of horsemen everywhere. *Win at Old Orchard, win the Hambletonian.*

And on the night after the National had been run off, history flaunted the words. On that night stunned horsemen read the headlines.

LASATER TAKES THE NATIONAL
LASATER, PILOTED BY SEP PALIN, BEATS ROSALIND
LASATER WINS BY A LENGTH AND A HALF
ROSALIND BOWS TO ED LASATER

Men at microphones tossed questions light and easy over the air, not knowing that in a car on the way to Goshen a man and a boy were listening, trying not to, as if the listening would admit the doubt.

Lose at Old Orchard, lose the Great Race?
Rosalind a fallen prodigy?
Rosalind a morning-glory?
The words came through the air into the car as it sped along

193

in the dark. They broke in brittle fragments about the man and the boy.

For days afterward the smile was gone from Ben White's face, and the weather creases seemed etched deeper. Gibson tried to comfort him. Over graham crackers and milk in the stable office, he spoke confidently. "We'll change that old battle cry, Dad, to 'Lose at Old Orchard, win the Hambletonian.' "

Mr. White tried his smile. "Rosalind seems to be sharp right now," he said. "Went a good trip this morning. You saw for yourself." He paused a moment, then went on, not wanting to build false hope. "But, Son, that Ed Lasater's tough. He's got a mark of two-two and a quarter now against Rosalind's two-three. Fact is," he added, breaking a graham cracker for Bear, "he's already equaled Greyhound's time in the Hambletonian last year. And he'll be piloted again by Sep Palin who drove Greyhound."

Gibson spoke half laughing, yet half serious. "At Old Orchard was the one time I forgot the rabbit's foot Mike gave me."

"Pooh!" answered Mr. White. "Who believes in good luck pieces?" Then his eyes twinkled. "But don't let me catch you without that rabbit's foot, come Hambletonian Day!"

Friends, relatives, acquaintances discussed Rosalind's chances, weighing them this way and that. Some were confident, with no mark of doubt between their eyes. Others spoke but could not look at Gibson. Even the Whites' friend, Governor Hoffman of New Jersey, tried to prepare the boy for Rosalind's possible defeat. He sat on the fence rail alongside him one day, stop watch in hand. "For sentiment, I'm picking Rosalind," he said, then hesitated a long time, "but a lion's apt to cross her path in Ed Lasater."

Twenty-Five

GOSHEN! August twelfth! Hambletonian Day!

The chugging of a train woke Gibson, throbbing in his head. The Erie, that was it. The same railroad that went through Chester. On this same road William Rysdyk had shipped his colt to the Union Course. Sharply awake now, Gibson held his watch to the light. It was long past six. Eight hours between this moment and the moment when the horses would parade to the post.

This was the uneasy time. The time of thinking.

"Ed Lasater's tough."

"Ed Lasater's the horse to beat."

"Lasater tied Greyhound's time in the Hambletonian!"

"Lose at Old Orchard, lose the Hambletonian."

"A lion's apt to cross her path in Ed Lasater."

"Ed Lasater's driver is good. He piloted Greyhound last year. Remember, Gib?"

"Morning-glory. Morning-glory. Morning-glory."

Words said yesterday, last week, the week before, kept probing like a dentist's pick, getting closer and closer to the nerve.

Gibson shook the thoughts out of his head. He got up, dressed quickly. "I just better not forget this!" he told himself as he took the furry little rabbit's paw out of the trousers he had worn yesterday and slid it into his pocket. Then he tiptoed past closed doors and out of the spacious house where he and his parents were staying.

The leaves on the old elm trees in the quiet street were barely stirring. No wind to slow the time, he thought as he walked to the restaurant where the drivers ate. But the drivers had eaten and were gone. Now the place was filled with tourists who had come to see the most famous race of the trotting turf. Whole families of them. Children swiveling on the counter stools, fretting to see the horses. Fathers and grandfathers who looked as if they had once driven horses of their own.

Gibson sat up at the counter, ordering little, eating little, forgetting he had seven and a half hours of waiting.

When he came out on the street again, a bright sun hit him full in the face. The track will be fast, he thought, walking quickly to get to it, through the crowd, across the town square, past the ivy-covered churches.

At the entrance to Good Time Park a friendly officer with more chins than he needed stopped Gibson. "No one allowed in this early," he said, aiming his finger as if it were a gun. Then he spied Gibson's badge with the word Owner on it. "Say!" he said, unbelieving, "you're not young Gibby White, are you?"

Gibson nodded, anxious to get inside, but the police officer grabbed his hand and shook it vigorously. "If your filly can beat that Lasater, she'll be Number One on my hit parade. Get along with you," he winked, pushing him gently through the gate. "And the best of luck to you."

Good Time Park was a buzz of activity. Tractors rattling by, harrowing and scraping the clay mile. Striped tents popping up like puffballs after a rain. Ladies in aprons decorating sawhorse tables to be filled with food.

"Gib!" One of the grooms spoke excitedly as he spied the boy. "The buckle on Rosalind's girth is got to be sewed. Your dad give me the keys to his car, and I got to drive over to a harness-maker in Montgomery and get it stitched. He says you're to come along and see the man does a good job."

Half an hour to Montgomery. An endless wait at the harness-maker's. The buckle sewed. Then errands not mentioned before. Little errands, but time-takers all. Lamb's wool and sponges to buy and salt refills. An owner to see.

It was late morning when all was done and they were back at Good Time Park. At the Ben White stable, men stood huddled around every stall but Rosalind's. Hers was empty. Without anyone's noticing him, Gibson went on out toward the track, where the drivers were warming up their entries for the big race. Like any railbird he perched on the fence, his eyes sifting and sorting the horses, then pouncing on the one he sought. He found her quickly. There was no missing her free action. No boots of any kind. No head pole. No side pole. No breast collar. Only the two-minute harness to match the two-minute mind. With a smile to himself he began liking her all over again, forgetting he had ever heard the name Ed Lasater.

Stride by stride he watched Rosalind, trying to make believe

197

this warm-up was no different from the others.

"Say, Bud," a young man sitting next to him asked, "how d'you tell the trotters from the pacers?"

"It's easy," Gibson answered. "The trotter's diagonal feet work in unison, but the pacer strikes out with both legs of one side at the same time."

"Oh. That's what makes 'em roll, huh?"

"Sure. That's why the pacers are called side-wheelers."

Yes, everything the same. Questions the same. And out on the track the same harrow scratching the clay and the same float smoothing it and the horses pulling out around them with the same unconcern.

Yes, everything the same. And yet it was not the same at all! A feeling of something about to happen hovered over and around Good Time Park. You could sense it. You could almost see it in the air, like heat waves rising.

A hand darted between Gibson and the man on the rail beside him. It was Guy Heasley's hand bringing letters and a telegram, and Guy Heasley's voice speaking. "Knew I'd find you here. Track's going to be lightning fast, ain't it?" Then he was gone without an answer.

Gibson slit open the telegram. It was addressed to Rosalind and read:

ROUGH WEATHER DELAYING TAKEOFF. KNOW YOU WON'T BE GROUNDED BUT WILL FLY AWAY TO VICTORY. MY BEST TO YOUR OWNER AND TRAINER.

DOC MILLS

There were letters too from Mike in Wisconsin and Beaver and Grubber in Norfolk. Gibson read them in the midst of the crowd with overtones of excitement all about him.

"We'll be tuned in," they said, "yelling for the driver in the black-and-white silks and the filly with the two white feet."

"Hey! Don't forget to hang onto my rabbit's foot!" Beaver underlined in black slashes.

At noon Gibson's mother came to the office of the stable with a picnic hamper filled with sandwiches and fried chicken and a thermos of cold milk. Gibson sat on the trunk, trying to eat, but the chicken that usually tasted so good had no flavor at all. It was strange to be in the busyness but not of it. To sit on the outer rim again, watching. For a moment he thought of the days when he had jogged Tony, and a kind of longing passed over him. At least then he had had something to do.

Clem McCarthy, the radio announcer, came in, talking and laughing with Mr. Reynolds. They accepted plates of food from Mrs. White. Suddenly Clem spied Gibson and put down his sandwich half eaten. "Gib! Will you help me this afternoon?"

"Who? Me? But what could I do?"

"You can help identify the horses and drivers. I'm all set up on the roof of the grandstand with some big telescope binocs and a loud-speaker. Will you be my spotter?"

"You mean you really need someone?"

Clem nodded vigorously. "You've grown up with these horses. You know their sires and dams, their trainers and drivers. You've got names at your fingertips. You're my man!"

199

Gibson's face lighted. At last he had something to do! "Sure I'll come." He picked up a drumstick and ate it with zest.

His mother smiled happily as she set a glass of milk beside him. He turned to her now. "There's a big ladder goes from the back of the grandstand up to the roof," he said. "You could make it up there, too, if you want."

Mrs. White looked pleased. "I'd like to, only it happens that your grandmother and Mrs. Palin and I have box seats. But really half of me will be on the roof with you and half will be with your father up behind Rosalind."

Mr. White came out of the dressing room now, splendid in his new racing silks with the creases still in them. He shook hands with Clem McCarthy.

Gibson waited to speak to his father alone, but two little girls in pigtails came shyly into the office and tugged at his jacket.

"Will you have to whip Rosalind in the race?" one asked timidly.

Mr. White spoke carefully. "When my son and I train a horse, we believe he gets to know what we want and tries to give us his best every time. A good horse doesn't have to be whipped. Rosalind will be just as anxious to be out in front as we are to have her. I'm sure she would suffer great shame if she were whipped for doing her best. Wouldn't you, little ladies?"

Satisfied, the girls nodded their pigtails and skipped out, eager to relay the words.

At last Gibson and his father were alone, but now that the chance had come, all the boy could say was, "Rosalind—?"

And all the father could do was nod. Neither had any words.

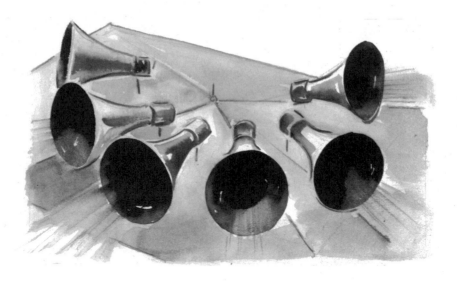

Twenty-Six

THE platform atop the roof smelled of freshly cut pine, and the sun drew out little gummy beads of pitch that stuck to Gibson's shoes. He wondered why he even noticed this when below him the grandstand was filling and overflowing to the rails. And beyond the rails Good Time Park spread out like some giant kite—the track itself the frame, the grassy infield, tissue-paper green. The roads to the park were black with cars. Miles of cars winding in the sun, worming down out of the darker green hills.

"How do you like the aerial view!" Clem McCarthy announced to Gibson rather than asked. He was all over the platform at once, testing connections, trying out his microphone, wielding the binoculars, tuning up for the begin.

For just a moment he perched on the rail of the platform and glanced at the script he drew from his pocket. "Say, Gib, how do you pronounce this driver's name? I always forget if it's Pay-lin or Pah-leen?"

"You pronounce it Pay-lin," Gibson answered quickly, eager to be of use.

Clem McCarthy nodded. Then his eyes swept the scene, gathering it into himself, distilling it for his listeners. Now he was bringing the microphone to his lips, talking into it, purring into it as if it were the ear of a beloved friend.

"Good afternoon, ladies and gentlemen, from Goshen, New York."

A battery of loud-speakers trumpeted the words with their in-held excitement.

"Post time," the voice rapped out, "is half an hour away but already the largest gathering in Hambletonian history has entered Good Time Park. Forty thousand lovers of the harness horse are milling about, waiting tensely. Five hundred horse celebrities are quartered here in the stables. Ten are now being harnessed for today's Hambletonian. One of the ten will win two out of three heats, and in the winning a new star will shine in the trotting firmament."

Gibson became part of the listening audience, forgot himself.

"Whoever," the voice ticked on, "thrills to the trot, to the pageantry of the turf, to the performance of a champion, is here today to pay homage to Rysdyk's Hambletonian. He, my friends, was the greatest of all progenitors of the trotting horse —the great-granddaddy of today's entries. This race is run every year in his honor."

A brush of wind picked up the flag over the infield and ribboned it to a cloud.

Again the voice with the excitement all boxed in. "The day is right. Warm but not too warm. Just enough breeze to send the colors rippling.

"The scene below us, ladies and gentlemen, could be a county fair. The church ladies are selling the last of their delicious fried chicken, corn on the cob, and homemade apple pie from their sawhorse tables under little mushroom tents. At least, they look like mushrooms from my crow's-nest here atop the grandstand. And part of every admission dollar taken in today, ladies and gentlemen, goes to the Goshen Hospital."

He crammed his script into his pocket, living the scene instead. "Today this quiet little land o' Goshen is a mecca. From country lanes, from city sidewalks, the crowd—" His sentence broke off in the middle.

Now the words rocketed. "The field is coming out on the track!"

Gibson looked at his watch. The waiting was over. This was it! Like a kaleidoscope the colors came. The silks of the drivers—purple, green, orange, scarlet, and one in sober black. But all the colors dimmed against the polished gleam of Rosalind.

"The entries," the voice quickened, "have drawn the following positions: Hollyrood Hermes in first place, Brownie Hanover in second, Gaiety Mite third, Recovery fourth, Pinero fifth, Clova in sixth . . ." The voice gathered speed like a plane racing its engines. "In seventh position Rosalind, owned by Gibson White, driver Ben Franklin White. Ladies and gentlemen, Gibson is standing right here beside the mike. He's going to help make individual horses out of the pack for you."

The voice never seemed to stop for breath. "In the second tier, behind the number one horse, is Ruth M Mac in eighth place, driver Tom Berry. Number nine, Peter Song behind Brownie Hanover. Number ten, Ed Lasater behind Gaiety Mite. Now they're going to score for the word 'Go.'"

Gibson only half listened. With heart and eyes he saw the field pass the judges' tower until they were a hundred yards beyond it. He saw them turn, saw the horses maneuvering into the positions they had drawn.

"Come on slowly!" It was the starter, Steve Phillips, cautioning from the track.

The lineup came at him, squaring off into a trot as they neared. "Stop! Go back!" Clem's voice cracked as two horses burst ahead of the number one horse and Steve Phillips clanged the bell.

Back they all went for another try.

Gibson hung onto the platform rail. "Don't let her wear herself out!" he prayed.

Again the field came at Steve Phillips. Again his caution, "Come on slowly!"

"Once more they're scoring for the word," shouted Clem McCarthy. "They may make it this time . . . Oh, no!" he cried in unison with the gong as one horse broke from his trot and leaped ahead of the pole horse.

A third try.

Fear caught at Gibson. The horses would surely be worn out before they took the word. Never Rosalind's fault, but taking something out of her just the same. He chafed at the feeling of being far away. He wanted to be down there among them, as if his just being there would bring order.

A groom with a bicycle pump came running out on the track. "Gib," whispered Clem McCarthy, "whose tire is flat?"

"It's Peter Song's," wailed Gibson.

"Ladies and gentlemen, everything can and does happen at a harness race. Peter Song's sulky has a flat, but stand by, we're on the job, pumping it up."

The minutes' delay loomed big and bothersome. But finally the tire was pumped and the scoring began again. On the fifth try the field worked with clock precision, starting at a walk, picking up the trot at the come-on signal, holding their positions as they hit the wire.

Now Steve Phillips was yelling "Go," the crowd yelling it with him.

It was a race!

Gibson saw Rosalind far on the outside of the pack, holding her position as if they were still scoring. His hands clenched. Why doesn't she go to the rail? Why doesn't she? His father's words came rushing at him: "Rosalind likes to *make* the pace."

Why isn't she doing it?

Why? Why? Why?

But as the field neared the turn and bunched, relief poured through him. Now he saw why. His father was driving a waiting first quarter! Holding her safe! Taking no chances! In a flash Gibson knew that if he had been driving he might have crowded for position, blocked himself in, lost the race in the first quarter. He was glad his father held the reins!

The words of Clem McCarthy drilled through the undertone of the crowd. "It's Brownie Hanover in the lead at the first turn. Rosalind moving in, opening up space. Now the way shows clear. Now Rosalind taking it, catching Brownie Hanover, whipping around him.

"Behind her Sep Palin pulling Ed Lasater wide. Wait . . . wait!" The voice dinned. "Number three is breaking into a wild gallop in front of Lasater. It's Gaiety Mite blocking him. Lasater's forced far on the outside now, straining to catch the field. He jumps into a break. Now Palin's getting him squared back onto his trot. He makes a good catch of it. But it may be too late, folks. They're at the half-way pole. It's Rosalind still on top by a length and a half. They're coming down the stretch now, Rosalind in the lead, Brownie Hanover in second place, Pinero third, Clova fourth. Now Ben White glancing back to see if anyone's closing in, but Rosalind's still two lengths out in front, her tail beckoning, 'Come on, Brownie! Come on, Lasater!' "

Gibson listened no more. Leaning out into space, his arms flailing, he was rooting his filly home, driving her in, stride for stride.

Eyes ahead, ears swiveled back to catch hoofbeats, Rosalind swept past the wire at her own pace.

"And what a pace!" Clem McCarthy's voice thundered as the timer hung out the mark on the timer's board. "Two minutes, one and three-quarters seconds! A half second faster than Greyhound's best heat last year!"

Forty thousand people were on their feet, jumping up and down, roaring, throwing hats high. And up above them a lone boy was sending his cheers to swell the tumult.

"Let the radio audience enjoy the roar of the crowd," Clem laughed as he caught Gibson and whirled him into a wild jig around and around the platform. Then, panting, he went back to the mouthpiece and poured everyone's excitement into it. "Gib White's bay filly took the lead at the first turn and was never headed. She led all the way, folks. All the way, to win by two lengths. She's a flying machine. Two minutes, one and three-quarters seconds for the mile."

Suddenly Gibson sobered. The second heat could be different. The race was not over. He saw the horses jogging back to the stables to blow out while another event took place.

He tried to watch the next race, a heat for pacers. Wood-enly he answered Clem McCarthy's questions. But in his mind he was at the stable helping with Rosalind, sponging off the sweat and dust, hand-rubbing her back and legs, offering her a few mouthfuls of water.

The second heat *was* different. Even from the beginning it was different. As winner of the first heat, Rosalind had the number one position now, and Ed Lasater was sixth instead of tenth.

This time only one false try and the horses were ready for the word. With the unity of boys at a track meet they came up to the wire, and passed the wire at the word "Go."

And away from the wire they went, trotting faultlessly, all ten of them. And there was Rosalind moving out in front, her two white feet and her two dark feet punching out in unison. Rosalind sweeping around the turn alone! Rosalind making the pace. Behind her, within striking distance, Pinero, Brownie Hanover, Ed Lasater, Ruth M Mac.

"At the half-mile pole, folks," Clem McCarthy was taking his listeners into his confidence, "Brownie Hanover is trying hard. He's collaring Pinero, nosing ahead of him. But wait! Ed Lasater's turning on his speed." A chill came over Gibson as he saw Ed Lasater working his way forward, moving up on Pinero, drawing away from him, moving up on Brownie Han-over, drawing away from him, moving up on Rosalind, chal-lenging her!

And then at the far turn came the clash everyone expected, the duel everyone had paid money to see!

Now Ed Lasater's muzzle was almost touching the black and white cap. He was pulling around Rosalind's sulky. Now his nose was even with her driver. Now he was at her flank. Now looking her in the eye! Gibson cupped his hand over his mouth as if all of him wanted to cry out.

"He's got her!" A thousand voices shrilled up from the stands as one voice.

"He's got her! He's got her!"

Gibson shut out the cries. He was down there on the far turn, in Rosalind's sulky, holding the reins over her, clucking, telegraphing, calling on her for the supreme effort.

And she was answering him, turning on her speed for him, inching away from Ed Lasater, widening the gap between them. By a quarter length. By a half length.

Behind her Sep Palin was pulling up on his reins, trying to lift Ed Lasater out in front. And behind him, the field. Whips lashing. Lines flapping. Drivers shouting. Only Rosalind's driver sitting tight, letting his horse alone, letting her do it herself.

"A solo finish!" shouted Clem McCarthy. "Rosalind two lengths in the lead."

Gibson looked at his stop watch as she crossed the line. Ed Lasater had forced her to go the last half in one minute, the last quarter in twenty-nine and a quarter seconds.

"Rosalind wanted to win!" he shouted. "She meant to win!"

There was no doubt about it. The big-going filly wanted all along to win.

Clem McCarthy's arm waved Gibson in toward the microphone, but the boy had to get out on the track. He had to! Two at a time he backed down the rungs while the loud-speaker boomed in his ears.

"It was Rosalind all the way. She was too much horse for Ed Lasater. Ladies and gentlemen, we promised you a new star this afternoon. Here she is. Her name is Rosalind."

Gibson landed running behind the grandstand. He had to thank Rosalind and his father. He tried to cut in and around the crowd, but they were a solid mass. Then someone recognized him, saw the look in his eye, made way for him.

And now he was on the track, in a cry of joy gripping his father's arms while forty thousand throats sent up a shout. That boy out there was doing what all the great throng wanted to do—take Benjamin Franklin White to their hearts. And their united arms took in the boy and the filly, too.

Even the thousands who believed in Ed Lasater were shouting themselves hoarse. Even Mr. Reynolds himself. And in a box in the grandstand Mrs. Palin was hugging Mrs. White, telling her it just had to be this way. Mrs. White wasn't able to answer at all. She was sobbing and holding onto her mother's hand as if she were a little girl again.

As Gibson ran back and forth in frantic joy between his father and his filly, neither could say very much because of the din. But Mr. White was thinking, "What a good dose of horse medicine Rosalind has been!" And he was wishing Dr. Mills were here to see.

In answer to his thoughts, a red-and-white plane came scudding out of the clouds, circling over the track, signaling with its wings.

"That must be Dr. Mills!" shouted Gibson.

Mr. White nodded, looking up. The plane was circling the track, going up, stalling, coming back down, motors roaring. He imagined he could hear Dr. Mills encouraging the pilot: "Go ahead. Do a loop. I don't care if my heart falls out."

And then Mr. White looked up into the sky beyond the wing tips. Into the blue silence he made his prayer of thanks to the Great Pilot, not for the race-win, but for the strong young arms that gripped his own.

By now camera bulbs were flashing, photographers tearing off pieces of black paper, letting the wind crackle them away. Rosalind shied from the frightening bits of paper, pulled her head toward the safety of her stall.

It was Guy Heasley who came to her rescue. With a proud and happy grin he led Rosalind to the stable, while her driver and her owner were escorted to the judges' tower.

The presentation of the trophy lasted only a few minutes. Yet everyone in that vast audience knew it had taken three years to make this moment.

"It gives me great pleasure," Mr. E. Roland Harriman, president of the Hambletonian Society, was saying, "to present this trophy to Gibson White, owner of the sensational filly who won today's Hambletonian.

"Rosalind," he said, "was named out of *As You Like It,* and that is how she won her race. She set a new record for the fastest time ever made by a Hambletonian winner. Somebody," the words boomed solemnly, "should write a book about Rosalind. Only no one would believe it!"

Gibson looked at the silver gleaming in Mr. Harriman's hand. And, wonder of wonders, it was not a cup, it was a tea set! A Hambletonian tea set! His eyes widened as he accepted it.

Now Mr. Harriman was paying tribute to Mr. White, calling him Hambletonian Ben, the grandest Roman of them all.

As the speech ended, the tea set was suddenly whisked out of Gibson's hands and replaced by a microphone. He looked at the shiny metal thing in awe. The very closeness of it was frightening. He tried to hand it back, but no one would take it—not Mr. Harriman, nor William H. Cane, president of the Goshen track, nor Mr. White. They just stood there laughing, nodding their heads at him, urging him to say a few words.

Gibson saw the dizzying crowd, banked until it met the platform on the roof. A new wave of fright washed over him. For a long second he stood with his hands frozen to the metal stem, saying nothing. Then a few little words began to form inside him. He said them out as they came.

"I'm the luckiest fellow in the world." He paused and began again. "I not only have a great filly. I've got a great dad."

There was a little stillness. The words were so simple the listeners expected something more. But no more came. And then the crowd took up the words and sang them back.

"A great filly! A great dad! A great . . ."

Twenty-Seven

AFTER the victory Gibson helped cool out Rosalind. She closed her eyes and relaxed as he walked her, sometimes nodding her head on his shoulder. And then she was back in her stall, rattling her empty feed tub as if she knew she had done her work well.

Guy Heasley bustled importantly over to Gibson. "Here's a handful of oats. Go on, Gib, give her a little appetizer. Then you better be readying yourself for the big horsemen's dinner."

Gibson took the oats, although his pockets already bulged suspiciously. He let Rosalind lip them from the palm of his hand, quietly watching his own reflection in her eyes. "You did it, Beautiful!" he said very softly when no one was looking.

Then he went out of her stall and around to the office. He found his father in shirtsleeves and his old hat, relaxing in a camp chair outside the door. A banty rooster perched on his knee, pecking at some corn kernels in his hand, and more banties scratched in the dirt at his feet.

Gibson sprawled down on the doorstep. "Dad," he asked, flipping some oat seeds to the banties, "do you feel like dressing up and going to a big dinner tonight?"

"Pshaw, no!"

"Could we—?"

"Could we what?"

"Could Mother or Grandmother make up something to eat and just the four of us go out to the Millers' place in Chester and have a picnic up there on the hill?"

Mr. White shoved his hat back and passed his hand across his forehead. He stretched out his legs, first one and then the other, and let his eyes close, remembering the peace of the spot. Then he sighed happily. "By George, I think the Millers would like it if we came to see them tonight. We could return Hambletonian's pedigree to them, too."

"And if they aren't home," Gibson suggested, "we could picnic anyway?"

"Like as not." Mr. White's voice had a kind of impatience in it. "But we'll have to wait an hour. Your grandmother is resting. You know, Son, she went two very fast heats this afternoon."

Gibson grinned. "Maybe that's part of the reason Rosalind won. Everybody was trotting with her. Hey, Dad!" His eyes lighted with a sudden idea. "We have an hour. A whole hour. I'll telephone Mom about the sandwiches for the picnic. Then I'll meet you in the car. Hurry, Dad!"

After Gibson made his telephone call, he came back and got in the car with his father.

"Well? Your mother like the idea?" Mr. White asked as he started up and drove past the deserted parking lot and out through the unguarded gate.

"She said she'd like nothing better. They'll be ready when we get back."

"Where do we go now, Son?"

"Across the Erie tracks and out toward Sugar Loaf."

"You figuring on making a kind of pilgrimage." It was more a statement than a question.

Gibson stole a quick glance at his father. "Why, yes."

"And where do we go in Sugar Loaf?"

"I don't know exactly. But there's a monument to Rysdyk's Hambletonian I'd like to see."

The car sped through the elm-shaded streets, then out on the back road to Sugar Loaf.

"They say there's two shrines." Mr. White spoke slowly, thoughtfully. "One on the Jonas Seely place where the colt was foaled, and a great big monument where he was buried over in Chester. Two shrines for the horse. None for the man."

"That's okay. William Rysdyk would prefer it that way."

Mr. White nodded. "I think he would."

"I don't want to see the big monument after all," Gibson said. "Let's go to the foaling spot."

Mr. White tossed his hat on the back seat. "Son, how is it with you? How do you feel?"

The blue hills in the distance, the quiet, winding road made talk come easy. Gibson drew a deep breath of happiness. "When Rosalind won, I felt just tops, Dad. Tops all over—as if I could trot a two-minute mile myself."

"I felt pretty good, too," Mr. White chuckled.

"Dad—?"

"Um-m-m?"

"Don't you think horses come to know when it's a workout and when it's the real thing?"

"No question about it."

"Then Rosalind knew?"

"She knew." Mr. White scratched his back against the seat in content. "It was a strange thing about this race, Gib. From the moment I climbed into the sulky and took hold the reins I knew we had a winner. I don't think any horse in the world could have beaten us today."

"And when Rosalind pulled away from Ed Lasater, I knew something, too."

"Meaning?"

Gibson laughed out. "I knew we had a champion on our hands!"

The tiptop of old Sugar Loaf showed itself now, dark against the sky. Gibson had half expected it to be white, like the sugar he fed the horses. A pheasant, flushed by the car, flew up from a tussock of grass.

Mr. White began humming a lazy tune, tapping out the rhythm on the wheel.

"With the purse Rosalind won," Gibson said, his eyes mounting with the bird, "I can finish paying for her training costs. And the rest of the money I'd like to use"—he paused, then blurted—"to go into business with you!"

The humming stopped. The hand on the wheel tensed.

"It's just as you said, Dad. Some day Rosalind will be a brood mare and I'll be driving her colts."

A silence that was good closed them in as the car climbed a slow mile. At last Mr. White could hold the gladness in no longer. He pulled off the road and stopped, even though they were in front of a farmhouse.

"I feel so good," he sighed, glancing across the road and up and up to the tower of the mountains. "Fact is, I could take an old horse like Pegasus, score for the word on the bald dome of Sugar Loaf, and drive right across that cloud lazin' over yonder."

"Hmpf," snorted Gibson, "with a colt out of Rosalind I could pull out around you and kick cloud dust all over your winged horse."

Mr. White's voice was far away. "There's another reason why I feel good," he said. "It's because you wanted *me*, not one of the younger men, to drive today."

A screen door scraped across a sill and a friendly voice called to them. "Were you looking for the Banker farm?"

Mr. White got out of the car and walked up to the house. "Strangely enough, we were," he said. "I understand the Banker farm used to be the Jonas Seely place. Are you Mrs. Banker?"

The woman nodded, brushing the flour from her apron.

Now Gibson was out of the car and on the bottom step of the porch. "Could we—would you mind if we visited the place where Hambletonian was born?"

"Why, not at all," she smiled. "We're glad to have folks interested."

Gibson liked her at once—not because she was prettier and less tired looking than most farm women nor because she smelled of a freshly baked cake, but because he thought he saw in her a pride in living on the same land Hambletonian himself had trod.

"Go on down the road to that cattle gate." She made a right-hand sign to them. "You can open it and drive across the pasture lot till you come to the marshy place. Then you'll have to foot it across a little log bridge. And there you are! The oak tree and the boulder with the writing on it."

When they had driven through the gate, Mr. White stopped. "I'm tired, Son. I'd like just to sit in the car with the doors open and smoke a cigar and rest my bones. Maybe even doze a little. You go on."

Underfoot there was a springiness in the quaggy earth. It would feel good to a crippled mare, Gibson thought, and to a colt's heels. He came to the footbridge and crossed it gingerly, wondering if these were the same logs William Rysdyk had laid. Then he went up a little rise toward an oak tree and found the place.

The present fell away, and all at once Gibson was in the heart of the past. Everything just as it had been. The grassy knoll for the colt's bed. The rugged boulder for him to scratch against. And the same wind saying "Sh!" in the oak leaves.

Yet there was a difference, too. Where before there were three oak trees, now there was only one. It was gray and hollowed but still making a brave show of green leaves and acorns.

Gibson went around the tree to the boulder. A small bronze tablet had been fitted into its face and on it the words:

HAMBLETONIAN
FATHER OF THE TROTTING HORSE
FOALED ON THIS SPOT
MAY 5, 1849

A woodpecker began drumming noisily on the hollow trunk of the old oak. The past faded under his hammering. A wet-nosed cow dawdled over, eyeing the quiet intruder.

Gibson looked about him, wishing he had some tribute to leave beside the boulder. He saw blackberries shiny and round on bushes nearby, and Queen Anne's lace growing wild, and huge acorns everywhere on the ground.

Nothing for him to give. Only things to take. Fruit to sample and acorns for keepsakes. He stooped down and picked up an acorn from here, one from there, until he had a handful. He might send them to Mike and Grubber and Beaver. He had never seen such acorns as these. How big they are! he thought. The tree seemed struggling to reproduce itself, to be immortal like the colt it had sheltered. He thrust the acorns into his pocket, among the spiky oats. Suddenly his fingertips were feeling the smooth, hard little kernels. "Oats!" he said softly. He cupped his hand, bringing them out. Oats were better than any wreath. Hambletonian and the Kent mare would have snorted in agreement. Oats would grow!

With a twig he scratched the soil around the boulder. Then he scattered the seed, walking once around, and once around again. From the edge of the ditch he picked up some clods of the peaty earth and broke them with his fists and let the crumblings fall over the seeds. Then with a sigh of satisfaction he started back to the car.

The sky was blue and deep with dusk now. Only one wispy white cloud overhead. Gibson watched it with a smile of wonderment. If he squinted his eyes ever so little, he could see in the cloud a human head strangely familiar—a rugged head with ears pointed a little at the top—the face of William Rysdyk smiling in his white beard. *Who else?*

ROSALIND
1:56¾.

and now . . .

I T TURNED out that Gibson and his father did have a champion on their hands. A world champion. Rosalind went on to become the fastest trotting mare the turf has known. In a match against time she earned a mark which no other mare has ever touched—1:56¾ for the mile.

In Gibson's black notebook he shows seven world championship performances for her, three of which have never been equaled: the three-heat record, the four-year-old record for the mile, and the all-age record for the mile. Today, as Queen of Trotters, she wears a triple crown between those forking ears—the Hambletonian, the Kentucky Futurity, and the Transylvania.

Even in a handicap race when she had to start more than two hundred feet back of the starting line, she overtook horse after horse and went to the front at the first turn. Then she breezed home, the winner. The greater the challenge, the more determined she seemed to win.

Only one trotter could better her mile record, and that was the mighty Greyhound, by a tick and a half. Between them, Greyhound and Rosalind took every race in stride. There were no records left for them to break.

Then someone had an idea. Why not hitch Greyhound and Rosalind pole to pole? The world champion trotter and the world champion trotting mare in double harness!

The idea caught on. And in the year 1939 the exhibition took place, with Sep Palin holding the lines. Time seemed to stand still as the King and Queen of the trotting turf flew around the track in great reaching strides. By four and a quarter seconds they shattered the world team record that had stood for twenty-seven years. Five days later they did it again, bettering their own record, lowering it to 1:58¼.

And now? What of Rosalind now? She is retired to the Blue Grass country of Kentucky, with a record of twenty-seven races won. But her career is by no means ended. She is a busy brood mare, raising colts for Gibson to train and drive. Three of her fillies have scores—Rose Dean, 2:04¾; Rosamond, 2:03⅗; and Deanna, 2:02¾, the fastest two-year-old of 1945.

Who drove them to their records? Why, Gibson White, of course. Long, lean Gibson. And with the sun glints in his eyes, he is still working to win the Hambletonian with a colt out of Rosalind.

For their help the author is grateful to

E. ROLAND HARRIMAN, president, The Hambletonian Society

WILLIAM H. CANE, president, Good Time Park, Goshen, N. Y.

JOSEPH S. COATES, designer of Good Time Park, Goshen, N. Y.

WILLIAM H. STRANG, JR., owner of two Hambletonian winners, The Ambassador (1942), Volo Song (1943)

MR. AND MRS. W. SANFORD DURLAND, Chester, N. Y.

MR. AND MRS. RICHARD K. MILLER, Chester, N. Y.

ROY MILLER, Lexington, Ky.

TOM GAHAGAN, turf scribe, Indianapolis

CHARLES E. KOONS, publisher, *Times Herald*, Middletown, N. Y.

EDWARD P. DOUGHERTY, editor, *Times Herald*, Middletown, N. Y.

THOMAS W. MURPHY, Poughkeepsie, N. Y.

DR. S. W. MILLS, Middletown, N. Y.

COLEMAN J. KELLY, turf consultant, Chicago

STEPHEN G. PHILLIPS, starter, Westbury, L. I.

CLEM MCCARTHY, radio announcer, New York, N. Y.

CHARLES W. HINKLE, radio announcer, Dayton, O.

GEORGE COOK, Netherlands Information Bureau

BENJAMIN HUNNINGHER, Queen Wilhelmina Professor, Columbia University

DR. HENRY J. VAN ANDEL, Calvin College

DR. ADRIAN VAN KOEVERING, Zeeland, Mich.

PROFESSOR NELSON VAN DE LUYSTER, The Citadel, Charleston, S. C.

WILLARD C. WICHERS, Netherlands Information Bureau

THOMAS S. BERRY, trainer, Lexington, Ky.

S. F. PALIN, trainer, Indianapolis

STANLEY STUCKER, reinsman, Stockton, Cal.

MRS. T. WAKELY BANKER, Sugar Loaf, N. Y.

C. H. BORLAND, Goshen, N. Y.

MISS MARY BRANHAM, Orlando, Fla.

MRS. WILLIAM FLEMING, Pinehurst, N. C.

MR. AND MRS. JOHN C. MEDRICK, Goshen, N. Y.

MRS. MARION B. RUTAN, Goshen, N. Y.

STAFFS OF *Harness Horse Magazine, Hoof Beats, The Horseman and Fair World, Chester News, Goshen Independent Republican*

BERTHA M. BORLAND, Goshen Public Library and Historical Society

H. H. HEWITT and ROBERTA SUTTON, Chicago Public Library

MILDRED LATHROP and FERN FINFROCK, Gail Borden Public Library, Elgin, Ill.

LOUISE KEUCK, St. Charles Public Library, St. Charles, Ill.

ELEANOR PLAIN, Aurora Public Library, Aurora, Ill.

AVIS GRANT SWICK, St. Charles, Ill.

EMILY B. WHITE, Lexington, Ky.

GERTRUDE B. JUPP, Milwaukee, Wis.

NICK SAUM, Wayne, Ill.

MR. AND MRS. L. C. FERGUSON, Oak Point, Hammond, N. Y.

CHARLES RUDERMAN, Gouveneur, N. Y.

SIDNEY CROCKER HENRY, Wayne, Ill.

MRS. KENNETH M. HESS, St. Charles, Ill.

DR. FREDERICK E. HASKINS, St. Charles, Ill.

EDWARD PACUINAS, horseman, St. Charles, Ill.

WILLIAM WINQUIST, horseman, Wayne, Ill.

HENRY YUNKER, countryman, Elgin, Ill.

and especially to Gibson White's mother
SARAH GIBSON WHITE